THE FLYING HORSE

ONCE UPON A HORSE

BOOK 1

ONCE UPON A HORSE

THE FLYING HORSE

SARAH MASLIN NIR

art by LAYLIE FRAZIER

cameron kids

Book design by Melissa Nelson Greenberg

Library of Congress Cataloging-in-Publication Data available.
ISBN: 978-1-951836-67-2

Printed in China

10 9 8 7 6 5 4 3 2 1

CAMERON KIDS is an imprint of CAMERON + COMPANY

CAMERON + COMPANY
Petaluma, California
www.cameronbooks.com

To the real Grandma Frieda.

—S.M.N.

Chapter One

TRENDY

It was one of those dawns full of stillness. Winter had just taken off her overcoat, but spring had not yet flounced in. There was the silence of songbirds who overslept, bundled under down and cozy. The birds seemed unwilling to wake and warble into the still chill morning air.

The little horse, however, was wide awake. Everything was just too exciting.

You too would find even that quiet, quiet morning thrilling—if it was your very first day on planet Earth. And indeed, the nut-brown foal, curled in a not-quite ball under tumbles of crisp straw, had just arrived here. And he was determined to see the world. He'd been scrabbling to stand for the better part of an hour, with little luck. If only he could make his body listen!

He took a breath. He needed a new strategy. Maybe just try two hooves at a time? With a heave, he scrambled his rear legs to a standing position and—aha!—held them there. Two of those wobbly, fuzzy sticks folded underneath him were suddenly uncrumpled. He was up!

Well, the back pair of legs were at least. The front half of his body still lay in the warm straw. But the brief sense of accomplishment the hours-old foal felt was fleeting. It was all so tiring. But he would not fall down again! Instead, half propped up, he took a breather.

In the still-dark corner of the big birthing stall, his mother was dozing. Olina's coat was several shades darker than her new son's. Her belly had been so round as she'd grown the foal inside her over the last eleven months that she'd more than earned her nickname around the farm: Cocoabean.

For Olina, it had been a long night, laboring over this, her maiden, or first, foal. Though it was hard work, she had been very quiet, and the baby was a few weeks early, so the humans who took care of her had not been expecting him; they were still asleep in their beds in the farmhouse at the top of the hill. They'd missed the arrival of the little furry jewel now struggling in the hay.

Olina had not been worried. Instinctively she had known what to do. She lay down at points to help him turn inside her, then stood when she felt the baby shift into the position foals must take to be born: nose pointed toward their toes, chin over their knees, hooves pointed forward. A perfect swan dive straight to Earth.

After her hard work, she had dozed off, standing, as horses do, and now turned her head to see what the commotion by her hooves was all about. Her long forelock fell halfway over a sleepy eye. She snorted. The little foal was determined to stand, even if his new body was refusing to cooperate. It seemed he had reached a compromise with it: His front legs were still curled beneath him, but his back legs stood. He lay flopped like a half-pitched tent, bum in the air, and the scrap of a tail protruding from his rear, flip-flipping. He didn't notice his mother approach. He was busy pondering his next move.

Olina reached out her muzzle to gently clean her new son with her tongue. The flicker of motherly pressure was too much for his wobbly muscles and sinews to handle. The back legs he'd worked so hard to straighten collapsed. The foal keeled over with a little frustrated puff of air that could only be described as a horse's version of "harrumph!"

If horses could laugh out loud, Olina would have.

Over the next several hours, the sun rose over the village of Luttelgeest, turning rosy the just-arriving leaves of the pear and cherry trees. Its glow slid over the fruit orchards till the branches were as red as the round, brick clock tower that presided over the town beneath its funny green copper hat. Its warmth seeped deep into the rich dirt, where thousands of tulip bulbs nestled just out of sight, excited for the spring. Tight little fists of plants, they drank it in. And while no one can be certain, there in the dark earth, perhaps the tulip bulbs were excited too. They had good reason to be: every day they were erupting into rows of color so bright it looked as if a great painter like van Gogh had left his palette in the fields.

The little foal knew none of this; he'd not yet seen the rich fields of the Netherlands, the land where he was born. Nor had he ever watched those pastures spill out across the province of Flevoland, where the farm of his birth lay between two gentle rises of hill. There in the stall where he was born, he'd never yet even laid his deep brown eyes on the sun. But he felt its pull.

And so as the world and the birds and the tulips woke up, the foal did his best to make sure he was ready for it. By the time the sunlight slanted over the Dutch door of the barn, he had mastered his four feet and gotten all his hooves underneath him (with a few falls and more silent mare laughs in the process).

But he was slowly figuring out this whole standing thing. When he wobbled, he flip-flipped his stubby tail for balance. When his new knees buckled, he swung out his legs and stood with his hooves in a triangle. Olina moved closer, careful now not to tip her son over, and he knew exactly what to do. He nosed up beneath her and took his first drink of mother's milk.

It was just then that the farmer arrived with a pail of morning oats for Olina. He swung open that Dutch door with a creak—and nearly dropped the bucket of breakfast. There before him was a little foal, arrived nearly a month early, already on all four feet, blinking at him.

"Ongelofelijk!" the man shouted in his native Dutch. Unbelievable! He stood rock still. Olina shoved her muzzle under the farmer's armpit to remind him that those oats would not eat themselves. He laughed and regained his composure, briefly, dumping the food into her trough. "Good job, my Cocoabean! You deserve it," he said, as he shook out the pail. He turned once again to stare, shocked, at the little, perfect foal.

"So early, and so ready!" he said after a long silence, rippled only by Olina's steady grinding of the oats over her teeth. Gingerly, he reached out a hand to gently touch the baby's trumpet-shaped muzzle. The creature flinched, then decided the man's hands smelled deliciously oaty. They smelled good. And plus, the touch was soft. As the farmer cupped his hand under the baby horse's muzzle, the animal leaned his chin into the man's palm with a teensy sigh.

"You know what you are? Arrived here first, before any of the other foals on this farm?" the man said, his sun-crinkled face breaking into a wide smile. The baby horse blinked. "A trendsetter."

Trendsetter. The foal thought about it. He had never heard human speech before and of course did not know human language—and would never truly know it, beyond the emotions that all creatures share. But something in the appreciative tones in the farmer's voice, the look in his face, but most of all, the kind feeling in his hands, felt exactly right.

Yes, the foal thought, as his tired, tiny legs began to sway, and he lowered his weary self once more to the soft hay.

I'm Trendsetter.

Chapter Two

SARAH

Three-thousand six-hundred seventy-one and a quarter miles away from that cozy barn in Luttelgeest, at exactly the same time that Trendsetter was flopping and wobbling in the hay, someone else was struggling too. On a distant shore, on the other side of the broad Atlantic Ocean, far out of sight from the tulips that would burst like flowery fireworks across the pastures of Trendsetter's farm, was a girl named Sarah. And just then, Sarah felt a lot like the little horse, called Trendy, was feeling at that very same moment: frustrated.

Trendy, just born, just wriggling to life, of course had no idea that there was a world beyond his stall at all. He certainly didn't know that one day he would end up in a place called New York City, in America—a place that, if it were possible to gallop there, would take a horse like him some twenty million canter strides to reach (19,392,880 strides to be exact!). He didn't know any other humans even existed beyond, of course, the farmer who loved his mama, Cocoabean.

One day, Trendy's life would become linked to Sarah's, even with as far away as their lives began. But just as no human can see their future unwind before its time, foals, as magical as they may seem with their extra-special velvet noses and broom-bristle manes, do not know their fates either. Sarah and Trendy were important to each other, but neither of them knew that yet.

But perhaps, if young Trendsetter had seen Sarah at that moment and watched her stumbling, trying, failing—just like him—the foal would have felt a little better about himself. It is important for creatures to know that all of us have a tough time, sometimes.

To be clear, there in her family's apartment in New York City, Sarah, a ten-year-old human girl, was of course not struggling to take baby steps in a pile of hay! She was muddling through something different. But it felt no less challenging: Sarah was trying to spell.

Sarah's long brown bangs flopped over her forehead as she glared at a tattered old book on her desk. Perhaps if she stared long enough at this, her enemy, this beat-up copy of *The Horn-Ashbaugh Fundamentals of Spelling*, it would run away in fright. She shook her head at the silliness of the thought, the fringe falling into her eyes. Sarah had given herself the shaggy cut a few days before. She was proud of it—even though her mother shrieked when she saw the choppy, uneven locks and made Sarah promise to never, ever, EVER, play hairdresser on herself again. The new 'do made her look more like her favorite show jumper, the Olympian Beverly Woods, the fourth grader thought, even if Beverly's hair was strawberry blond. A poster of Beverly hung on the wall above Sarah's desk, right above the book she hated so. Sarah took her eyes off the book and looked up at the glossy image. Her scowl gave way to a smile.

Astride a chestnut Australian thoroughbred named Amigo, Beverly's look of determined concentration was matched exactly by the look on her horse's face. In the picture, the pair were sailing over a jump at the Olympic games in Atlanta, Georgia. The competition was called a Grand Prix. (Sarah's friends at Green Fields Stables, the barn she rode at on the weekends, had taught her that and how to pronounce the last word properly as "pree"—just like they would say in France). She had learned that the jump that seemed skyscraper-high towered at five foot three inches. Sarah was tall for her age, and she always had to stand awkwardly in the back row on class picture day. But that jump was taller than she was!

Sarah sighed then, much like Trendsetter sighed at that same moment on the other side of the world, contentedly snuffling underneath his mother for his milk breakfast. Looking at the picture made the girl feel better. She loved the pair so much that last Hanukkah she had begged her parents for a model horse of Amigo, crafted exactly like him by a company called Breyer, and now the perfect one-to-eight scale replica of the chestnut sat beneath the poster on the edge of her desk. It was her prized possession. She reached out and stroked Breyer Amigo's smooth plastic flank. If Amigo and Beverly could do something *that* impossible, if a horse and a human together could fly, surely Sarah could tackle *The Horn-Ashbaugh Fundamentals of Spelling*. Right?

But words always danced across the page when Sarah looked at them, a problem she had been keeping secret from her mother and father, and even from Grandma Frieda. Squint and stare at the page as hard as she might, the letters always got all jumbled. Consonants and vowels seemed to tangle like the legs of a colt who tries to race the butterflies flitting across the field and ends up in a stumble-scramble because he didn't watch where he put his hooves.

She couldn't possibly tell her family about her predicament. Sarah's mother and father were writers. Even Grandma Frieda was good with words, showing Sarah how to click-clack them out on an antique Sholes and Glidden typewriter. The hulking machine was what Grandma had used to type up her work when she had been a secretary, just like Sarah used her computer, she explained, during one of their weekly Sarah-Grandma hangouts.

Grandma Frieda was where Sarah had gotten her love of horses, even though her grandmother had never had any horses of her own. She was from Austria, which she called "the old country," and her family had been very poor, with barely enough money to afford to eat. They lived in the city of Vienna, and way back then, milk was delivered every morning, because no one had a refrigerator to keep it cool and fresh. Each morning, the milkman would come by at dawn with his delivery, and it was little Frieda's job to hand him an Austrian schilling and collect the milk.

Though the milkman certainly came early, Frieda always beat him to the corner where they met. That is because pulling the milk cart was a palomino pony. Frieda would always save a crust from her supper to feed to the little pony. The pony's name was Modisch, and challah bread was her favorite. The milkman was moved by Frieda's generosity—he knew the little girl herself had so little to eat—and so once a week he would gift her a jug of cream. The extra food was a blessing for her family, and her mother would smother Frieda with kisses every time her daughter returned tottering under the weight of the jug.

And so it was that Sarah's grandmother, from a very young age, linked horses with goodness, plenty, and pleasure. Modisch the pony, pulling her little cart, brought joy to Frieda's family. But in truth, to Frieda, it was the pony herself who was the true delight, and she would have loved her and cooed over her as she jingle-jangled her wagon past Frieda's home whether or not sweet cream came along too.

Sarah-Grandma hangs were when Sarah felt she could be most herself. When the smell of frying potatoes would somehow take away the rough day at school, the icky feelings of being too tall, too loud, and too bad at spelling. While Grandma cooked, she would plunk her granddaughter at the Sholes and Glidden and recite a story from the old country or a poem like her favorite, about a gray pony, for Sarah to click out across the keys. As Sarah typed, Grandma spoke, and she would slice a thick, white potato superthin, dropping each slice into a pan of hot oil. Grandma Frieda called the crunchy slivers "pony prints." The golden circles reminded her of the shape of the palomino pony's footfalls in the Vienna snow.

I had a little horse.
His name was Dapple Gray.
His legs were made of cornstalks,
his body made of hay.
I saddled him and bridled him
and rode him off to town.

Up came a puff of wind
and blew him up and down.
The saddle flew off, and I let go.
Now didn't my horse make
a pretty little show?

But that evening, as Grandma had recited the second line in the first stanza, Sarah recalled, her fingers had hovered above the keyboard. Dapple. D-a-p-p. She was unsure of what letter to press. Her mind fluttered, just as it did when she couldn't spell a word at school. As she struggled to pin down the spelling—did the *l* come before the *e* or the other way around?!?—a wave of unkind thoughts rushed over her. She must be so very stupid, Sarah thought to herself, to not know how to spell a word she used all the time.

There was a silvery pony at the barn where she rode, Green Fields Stables. The gray whorls on his white coat were called dapples, her instructor had told her, and Sarah loved that they looked like snowflakes sprinkling his fur. That very same evening, as Grandma peeled the potatoes for their treat, Sarah had told her stories about the sneaky little pony. How his eyes seemed lined in black eyeliner like a movie star, and his nose had a pink dot at the tip, as if he dipped it in Grandma's favorite strawberry ice cream. She told of the day that the pony had bellied down to reach for clover under the planks of the pine fence that kept him safe in his paddock and figured out he was small enough to wriggle out entirely.

Grandma had laughed as Sarah told her how the escapee was discovered hours later, hiding out amid a herd of brown Jersey heifers who were pastured down the road. The silver pony was doing a very bad job at pretending to be a cow. "Especially a brown one!" Sarah said as Grandma roared.

Dapples. Only now, the spelling wouldn't come.

Sarah tapped out D-a-p-p-. The typewriter thunked each letter onto the rolled-up sheet of paper. She stopped. She couldn't bring herself to tell Grandma that she was confused. She couldn't bear to have Grandma think of her the way the teachers at school did. They all told her she wasn't trying hard enough to learn the words. But Sarah knew she was trying with all her might.

"Grandma," Sarah said. "I think the typewriter is broken. It won't type the letters *e* and *l*." The shame at lying to her grandma burned so bright in her that she tossed her head, trying to hide her eyes behind her new bangs.

"Oh, really?" Grandma said then, flipping a slim potato from her spatula back into the frying pan with a little *splosh*. "Well then, come sit by me in the kitchen, and tell me more about that rascal, the silver-dapple pony," Grandma had said, dishing some crisp potato pony prints onto a plate lined with paper towel to cool. Sarah quietly breathed a sigh of relief. No one knew her secret, still, she thought. "Then after dinner we can have some strawberry ice cream."

That memory—the mix of guilt she felt at fibbing to Grandma and the warm feelings of being with her favorite person on Earth—floated around her as she sat at her desk. She was still facing her poster of Beverly Woods, *The Horn-Ashbaugh Fundamentals of Spelling* still unfortunately right in front of her. She'd do almost anything to replace that dog-eared book with a bowl of strawberry ice cream!

"If wishes were horses, we'd all ride to town," Grandma had said to her once. The message in the old-timey saying was that wishing for something doesn't get you anywhere. The way to get to town was to start walking—yourself.

Sarah cracked open the book. It was a lesson on double consonants. "When adding a vowel suffix (e.g., -ing or -ed or -er) to a word that ends with a single vowel followed by a single consonant, we double the final consonant. Example: wet: wetting, wetted, wetter." Sarah's head swam.

At that very moment, though she couldn't know it, more than nineteen million galloping strides away from her desk in New York City, a little horse she'd never met finally stood up for the first time ever. He flip-flipped his stubby tail. On her side of the world, Sarah straightened her shoulders. She took out her paper, and her pen, and copied down the first word in the double-consonant exercise:

T-R-E-N-D-S-E-T-T-E-R

Chapter Three

TRENDY

It was a fair May day in Luttelgeest some three years later, though the horses couldn't be sure of the month, measuring time as they do by things other than minutes, seconds, and hours. For horses, the passing of time—if it is measured at all—is not watched by a clock or a calendar.

For them, seasons do not have things like months; they have sensations. Time passes in the crisping of hay, all mown up from its once-green stalks. When it sits rolled into bales, yellowing in the sun, soon to be fodder, that means summer is over. The lick of frost on the grass underfoot. When it is crunchy where a short time ago was springy softness, winter is nearly here. The call of birds, the startle of wood creatures rushing to gather nuts, when before they played in the forest, without hurry, means autumn has arrived.

And on this day in Luttelgeest, horses sensed this time of year in smells. Bees toiled in the tulip field, gathering pollen and tucking it up in the little pouches on their hips. They hustled it home to the hive to make honey. The busy insects kicked up flower dust and the scent of blossoms as they buzzed over Trendsetter's barn.

Spring! Trendy thought to himself as he sucked a big draft of air through his nostrils, tipping his trumpet nose up to catch every delicious sniff. This is spring, the best of all seasons. His favorite. He nosed the air again. Flowers. Freshness. Spring. He whinnied with delight.

In fact, it was exactly three years later, by the strict human measurement that crams twenty-four hours into every single day—no less and not one more allowed—and 365 of those days precisely into a year. It was, according to people, 1,095 days since Trendy's first wobbly day in his stall, at the barn, and on planet Earth.

It was May 16. It was Trendsetter's third birthday.

Over the past three years (or as Trendy and his kind thought of them, over the past thousand moonrises, dawns, cool nights, and warm mornings) a lot had happened, even in Trendsetter's quiet barn. Most exciting was that he had three new best friends.

Three more foals had been born to Cocoabean's sisters at the farm in Luttelgeest the month after Trendsetter. Now a total of eight horses—four mares and their four children—peered out over the stall doors for their oats every morning. They whickered softly to the farmer with his pail, the horses saying in their horse way, "Give me breakfast first!"

The farmer understood their language quite clearly, despite not being a horse. Being a very fair man, he rotated his rations among stalls, so as not to play favorites. One day he'd choose first the gray mare and her jet-black son, Falkor, to have breakfast before the others; the next day it would be the small, reddish chestnut with the blond, or flaxen, mane and her identical little girl, or filly, named Willow. Then another morning it was the roly-poly pony mare and her bitsy baby, Kismet, who got their bran mash first.

The best day of all—at least in Trendsetter's opinion—was when Trendy and Cocoabean's troughs were filled before everyone else's. (Falkor, Willow, and Kismet strongly disagreed!) Today was one of those excellent days because it was Trendsetter's birthday.

Horses don't celebrate birthdays—or perhaps a better way to say it is that they are always celebrating as if it is their birthday. Each morning is a reset: a day to wake up, shimmy the dust off one's fur, flick the wood shavings out of one's tail, and take on what comes. Hopefully, that includes oats. Then it is to pasture, to delight in nature, chase butterflies and bunnies, forage for clover, bathe in dust, or bolt off nowhere in particular just for the sake of doing it. Trendy didn't keep time, didn't tick off days in a calendar, and didn't know it was his birthday. But more importantly, he didn't care it was his birthday. To a creature as perfectly in the moment as a horse, every day is just as good.

The farmer had different ideas, however, and that day, he decided that the calendar date meant that Trendy had grown up. Truly, he had been born early, hence his name, and was a year older than Falkor, Willow, and Kismet. All that bran mash, good clover, and tawny hay had made him stout like a drum. He was suddenly a lot bigger than his three still-babyish barn mates. Only his forelock hadn't grown much: It would remain stubby his entire life. But he was not a foal anymore. Trendy was now a young horse.

And so that morning, after Trendsetter had licked clean his bucket of breakfast (and, if we are honest, gnashed his teeth a bit rudely over the rim to make sure everyone in the stables got the message it was his snack, and his alone), the farmer did not lead him to the paddock with his three friends as usual.

The man had decided that Trendsetter was getting too big to romp and charge with his buddies safely; in fact, he was so large that the farmer thought he might accidentally bump into his playmates and knock them down.

Today, for the first time, he was turned out alone into a larger paddock next to his friends. The four youngsters were startled to be separated. Horses are herd animals, and unlike humans who sometimes like to curl up alone, to relax and recharge, horses are not naturally built to be solo. Once upon a time in the wild, Trendy's ancestors had to worry about predators who tried their hardest to get them. The safest place to be, when lions and tigers and hyenas wanted dinner, was in the warm folds of a giant herd. Galloping with an army of animals just like them, horses no longer had to be scared.

Of course, there is no such risk of a hungry predator to a horse who lives in a barn surrounded by tulip fields and under the shadow of gently creaking windmills. But that feeling of being happiest in a herd is still in the bones and cells of every single horse, even if stabled in a living room! So it was no surprise to the farmer that all morning Willow, Falkor, and Kismet stayed close, huddling with Trendy next to the fence that separated them. For hours they stood, and they stretched—the jet black, the flaxen, and the tiny pony foal—over the planks that reached to their chins trying to touch muzzles with their former companion.

U

Though his field had everything he could ever dream of—a bale of hay *all to himself*, clover and fescue grass that no other baby horse had yet snacked on or stepped on—Trendy wished hard to be on the other side of that fence, with his buddies. But after a few hours, the group settled down and decided that mowing the grass with their teeth, as long as everyone grazed right beside the fence line, was nearly as good as being together. Eventually, even with Trendy in his big-boy paddock and the babies in theirs, it was yet another great day to be a horse.

That is, until lunch.

With a jangle, the farmer strolled up to the paddock's edge, three metal buckets of oats thwacking against each other as he walked. Trendy, like all horses, could not count. So he did not notice that one bucket was missing.

Thus, Trendy remained calm as the farmer unlatched the gate of the pasture next to his and clipped it closed behind him. He was meek as a lamb as the farmer walked the oat pails to where his three friends stood, then hooked each on a fencepost. He slashed his black tail a bit when the three began stuffing their faces with oats without him, but Trendsetter managed to soothe himself: He'd soon have oats just as he did every day. Surely? Plus, once the oats were served to him solo, he wouldn't have to glare at anyone trying to steal his delicacy. Trendy may have not liked being pastured alone, but oooh, it would be good to be alone with oats.

"Ah, my big Trendsetter, time for grown-up feed for you, none of this kid stuff and lunch pails anymore, big man," the man said as he passed Trendy in his pen, reaching up to scratch the white star, that spot shaped like a diamond between the horse's eyes. "From now on, you'll get nutritious pellets for breakfast and dinner only—just like the show horse yer gonna be. But don't worry, boy; it's a double scoop."

Trendy, being a horse, did not understand the man's words. What he did understand was body language. He watched with a kind of horror as the farmer turned on his heel and headed back to the barn to fetch the adult horse feed. Trendy did not know that. All Trendy knew was THE FARMER DID NOT LEAVE OATS FOR TRENDSETTER.

It was probably the most tragic moment in the sheltered young horse's life. Trendy gnashed his teeth. He flattened his ears, a horse's version of a deep frown. Unlike humans, who share their emotions on their faces, smiling or scowling with crinkles around the eyes or eyebrows, horses don't show feelings in their eyes or on their lips. But their ears—that's a different matter.

31

All day long a horse's ears helicopter around, waving to and fro, cocking back, popping forward. The positions send messages loud and clear—if you know how to listen to ears. Here's a glimpse: Ears that flop to the side signal boredom, or perhaps daydreams of chewing on tulips or beating those darn butterflies in a race at last. Ears that tip back signal irritation, the kind of ears Cocoabean saw on Trendy's head whenever she used to sneak a bite of her son's breakfast. Pricked forward is a horse's smile.

Trendy was not smiling now. His ears were so flat back that their tips pressed to the fuzzy crest of his mane; then he smooshed them back a little more. Lunch for everyone in the farm—except him? Trendy. Was. Mad.

Angry little horses don't yell and scream or argue and insist. They don't have a lot of options at their disposal, really, except to dance out their feelings. They can leap skyward to express their frustration. Or arc their back and kick out their back hooves—that's called a buck. If the circumstances are seriously maddening, a horse might lift their front legs too. Doing this at the same time as kicking up heels in a buck is an acrobatic move called a crowhop. It is called that, perhaps, because for a few seconds the arching, kicking, striking animal is airborne, like a bird.

That afternoon Trendy tried it all to show the farmer how unjust the lunchless crisis was: He hopped, he skipped, he bucked, and he crowhopped until he was a blur of young horse bouncing around his paddock like a rubber dodgeball pinging around a gymnasium. In short, Trendy had a tantrum. It didn't bother the farmer in the least; he'd raised many young horses and knew that changes were tough, as they are for all creatures, and that everyone needs to express their feelings once in a while.

In the other pasture, Willow, Kismet, and Falkor didn't pay Trendy much mind. After a few startled snorts, the trio went back to snacking, their ears gently flicking as they chewed. The foals relaxed because they had realized something important: despite Trendy's insistence their lunch should have been his, their feed buckets were not at the slightest risk. That tall pine fence stood between them and Trendy's furious dancing.

At about the same time that the trio realized this, Trendy came to an opposite conclusion: Those feed buckets were not safe from him at all.

You could say that here in Trendy's young life emerged his first truth. It was one of those life lessons that we all learn and keep learning—if we're lucky enough to stay open to the truths of the world. That is not always possible. Sometimes, when hard times come, as they always will, as we grow into big horses or adult humans, it's a challenge to stay open to learning. One day you may feel that you know everything. Or maybe even, if those hard times pile up and crust over, you may feel that there is nothing more worth learning anyway.

Well, horses know that that is never, ever true. Horses are born curious and always strive to learn, and they know that there is always more truth out there.

Trendy's first truth went a bit like this: You are stopped only by what you can't get past.

It was up to Trendy to be the solution. The pine fence itself was not barring Trendy from the delicious oats on its far side, he reasoned. It was the little horse doing nothing about it that stood between him and those scrumptious buckets. And so, one, two, three, four, he dragged each hoof backward in the paddock dirt, reversing into its farthest corner. He lowered his head, he flick-flicked his still-stubby tail. AND THEN HE RAN LIKE MAD right at the tall pine fence, bunching each muscle in his growing flank, gritting his thick molars, clenching his jaw, and arching the crest of his neck . . .

He landed in a puff of dust—Trendy had leaped to the other side.

The foals jerked their heads out of their buckets. He was in their paddock now! And then, because there didn't seem to be any other course of action to take in the face of such a formidable horse, they each stepped aside and let Trendy eat up all their lunch.

Just then the barn door creaked, and the farmer stepped back into the yard. He looked from the empty pasture to the towering pine fence to the paddock with four young horses where there should have been three. For the second time in this horse's short life, Trendsetter caused the man to stop short in his tracks.

"Trendsetter!" he fairly yelped. "You can fly!"

Chapter Four

TRENDY

Koninklijk Warmbloed Paardenstamboek Nederland. Trendy looked up at those words, printed on a bright orange banner. It fluttered outside the window of the horse box in which he stood. He didn't understand what any of it meant, not in the least because he was a horse who can't read language, but because at that moment, he felt very, very lost.

It had been an hour's journey south from the only place he had ever known, the farm in Luttelgeest with his mama and his pals. He'd spent the last hour bouncing and hurtling down the road loaded up in what seemed to him like a stall on wheels, a brightly painted truck designed to haul horses. It was

December, just over six months after his big victory with the oats on his birthday, or, as Trendy thought of it, the time-when-the-tulips-hide.

Snow was falling outside of the van's windows, and a little had collected on the ledge nearest to Trendsetter. It was thick, a rare sight in the Netherlands; fine frosts were all Trendy had seen so far in his three and a half years. He darted out his tongue to sample it—and as quickly popped it back in his mouth. *Ptthhhhbt!*

The snow was so cold it tasted almost spicy, like the holiday cookies the farmer's children called pepernoots. They were sharp with cinnamon and cloves, and he loved when the farmer's son and daughter would sneak them to him in their pockets after their own supper. It was always a little sad to say goodbye to the cheerful tulips until spring roused them once again with her warmth. Pepernoot season made it bearable.

A pang pierced Trendy's stomach, but it wasn't for crunchy pepernoot. He was as far from his home as he had ever been, miles and miles from the red brick clock tower and its funny green copper hat. Olina was so far off he no longer could catch her comforting scent. And something in how the farmer had packed up the horse box—with the thick woolen horse rugs that Trendy would need only in much deeper winter—told Trendsetter he wasn't coming home for pepernoot season. If at all.

At the sight of the orange banner, in the driver's seat of the horse box, the farmer braked. He turned the clunky truck underneath where the cloth hung across a long driveway, spanning between two elm trees. Trendy braced himself against the motion, throwing his legs out in that same triangle that not so long ago had helped him stay upright as a brand-new foal. The vehicle came to a stop. Sunlight and globs of snow swirled into his stall as the door opened, and the horse squinted in the sudden brightness, a flurry of snowflakes collecting on his long eyelashes.

"Koninklijk Warmbloed Paardenstamboek Nederland, my Trendsetter!" the farmer read from the sign as he lowered the ramp from the trailer to the icy cobble road. As he spoke, his warm breath puffed into the chilly stall, reminding the little horse of how his mother would breathe over him to tell him he was with her and safe. He settled a little and blinked away the snow. "See that sign up above, boy? It means 'Royal Warmblood Studbook of the Netherlands,' my impressive jumping bean!" he continued. "That is what you are, a Dutch Warmblood—a K.W.P.N.! And here is where we will get you added to the history books—to the studbook, the official record of the most talented K.W.P.N. horses, like your grandfather Nimmerdoor! We will show the world how you can fly!"

To be a Royal Dutch Warmblood, a K.W.P.N., the most elite of the cool-minded and strong-bodied type of horse known as a warmblood, is tough. More than 450,000 horses live in the Netherlands, and eleven thousand foals like Trendy are born every year. Every single winter, nine hundred young male horses, called stallions, gather here, where Trendy in his horse box had just arrived, the city Ermelo, at the Nationaal Hippisch Centrum, the National Equestrian Center.

The National Equestrian Center was about to host an important event called the keuring. *Keuring* means a test, and Trendsetter was about to be seriously tested: Tomorrow was the yearly exam for all young Dutch Warmbloods. Trendy and the 899 other young stallions would spend the next thirty days proving that they were fast and fleet, sound and serious, and athletic and willing before panels of expert judges. Those judges would select just twenty-five of the top performers to move on to an even more rigorous test that would last one hundred days more.

The goal was to be selected by the panel as a top stallion, to earn a place in the Royal Dutch Warmblood Studbook. With that honor came the title of "preferent"—the best of the best. Trendy did not know this, but his grandfather, Nimmerdoor—nut brown like him but with a bright white stripe from eyebrow to muzzle where Trendsetter had a bright star—had earned this rare honor.

Out of the nearly nine hundred horses that enter the keuring each year, only about twelve are admitted to the studbook. Even fewer earn that coveted title. As the farmer unloaded his horse from the trailer, hooves gently crunching into the snow, he whispered into the horse's winter-fluffy ears. "Preferent," he said with a puff of steam into the cold air. "Preferent."

Winning that title was particularly important to the farmer for a secret reason: Times were tough, and the truth was that he could barely afford the hay he fed Trendy's mother and his friends. If his home-bred foal became a legend, Trendy would be valuable. Such a horse would be sold to a wonderful new home, and the farmer would be rewarded handsomely, filling his pockets with enough euros to save his farm.

Farmer and horse strode down the white drive to the red brick halls of the National Equestrian Center. The farmer's hands on the lead rope trembled with the hope that Trendsetter would carry on Nimmerdoor's legacy.

Trendy hoped that wherever they were going, there would be oats.

◡

That month, Trendsetter worked harder than he ever had worked in his brief life. He jumped obstacles that made the pine fence at home look as small as a thimble. He jumped without anyone on his back, galloping down a chute made from tall boards on either side. It was designed so that when his handlers urged him forward, he had nowhere to go other than toward the jump that towered at the end of the funnel of fences. At first it was daunting; he'd only ever jumped for oats before.

But the feeling of whoosh, pow, and crack urged him on; the takeoff, the soaring, the curling of his front legs and the arching of his back in the air, head pointed down like an arrow to the earth, became intoxicating. Soon Trendsetter was jumping for joy.

The judges watched. They frowned tiny frowns of concentration as they observed him gather himself up, so much like Nimmerdoor so long ago, and then fire off from the dirt. They'd scribble into their notebooks about his form, and his potential, and then stop writing. Because then, as the young horse soared in the air, he was suddenly completely different than his grandpa. Their pencils fell to the floor.

Trendy was better.

All the horse knew was that this new chapter of life was challenging but enjoyable and maybe even more so than blasting after butterflies across the field. He couldn't quite name exactly what made this experience—inside the big brick building of the National Equestrian Center, within its vaulted riding arena, out on its white dust rings with the rows of bleachers on each side—so stimulating.

Surely life back in Luttelgeest was full of delights. He thought of lipping Willow's mane as they stood side by side in a pasture, so that she would mirror him and scrape her small teeth along the crest of his neck where he couldn't reach, getting all the itchy spots so that his lip curled in satisfaction. He remembered racing Falkor, bouncing and bounding until their mothers whickered for them to calm down so they wouldn't hurt themselves. He thought of nipping the teensy tail of infant Kismet just to hear his pony whinny of protest. Missing here were the comforting sounds of home, like the clang of the clock in its tower. And he missed the tunes the tulip pickers hummed and the way that sound blew in with the breeze over the snipped flower fields and sang him to sleep in his stall.

Here at the Nationaal Hippisch Centrum, those pleasures were replaced with discipline; with working hard toward a goal; with waking early, eating right, and galloping off to complete a task. And though there were fewer butterflies dancing about this life, Trendy found it somehow more satisfying than his old pasture hijinks.

But not better than oats!

Chapter Five

TRENDY

"That's the star, over there, the one that's the new Nimmerdoor but—you won't believe it—an improvement on the original!" one of the judges said. She was walking through the barn with her clipboard and notebook, pen in hand. Trendy was used to such inspections by now. He had passed the first month with applause, and today he watched out the small window in his stable as horse boxes pulled into the courtyard, making tire tracks through a fresh blanket of snow. Around him horses were led from their warm stalls into the frost to board the trucks, a dusting of snow clinging to their manes like sugar. These were the young stallions who had not succeeded. They were headed home, perhaps a bit crestfallen, but to buckets of warm bran mash that would help with any hurt feelings. It took long hours to clear everyone out, but soon just two dozen stallions remained. The barn echoed with the absence of the horses Trendy had only just befriended, who now remained only as tire tracks in the snow.

"This one with the star—they call him Trendsetter. Isn't that cute? He is one of the talented few moving on to the second phase, the one-hundred-day keuring," the judge said. She was speaking to a woman wearing a hat that Trendy thought quite ridiculous. According to Trendy, all hats were preposterous because he couldn't quite understand the need for anything to be plopped on a head, ever. So you know it must have been funny looking indeed.

Trendy's dislike of hats was years old. Once, as a foal, Trendsetter had mushed his whole face into a feed pail. Crammed like that, he found himself stuck; with a leap backward, he had not managed to free himself from the pail but, rather, only to wrench the bucket from its hook on the wall. It was on his head still! For the next few minutes, the colt could do nothing but bumble around the stall, in the dark, stuck with this bucket-almost-hat on his head.

Cocoabean had long ago vowed to never again laugh out loud at her son as she had the day he was born, no matter his silliness. (And he was a very silly young thing, so this was very hard.) So she had to stifle her nickers of amusement as she watched her son wobble around, blind, with a bucket on his head. Finally, with a nudge from his mother's muzzle, the bucket popped off, leaving little more harm than some oats in Trendy's ears. Trendy disagreed. He was very offended by the bucket and blamed it, not his own greediness, for his predicament entirely.

After that, Trendy thought all hats, even the important hardhats his riders wore for safety, were very, very goofy. And this woman's hat was even more so, Trendsetter thought, eyeing it over the Dutch door of his stall. It looked like a helmet, but on either side of the head, each corner turned up like the floppy ears of the farmer's cocker spaniel, Hero, when he frolicked. The woman wore white britches and a coat the color of a muddy field when the tulips are hiding. Behind her, the jacket flared out into two darts that trailed behind her like Trendsetter's own tail did.

At Trendy's stall, she stopped and reached over the half-door as if to tousle the young horse's forelock. It had been thirty days since Trendy had seen his friend the farmer, and in that time none of the exercise riders or judges or trainers had offered gentle hands toward him. He missed that feeling. No one was harsh, but here at the keuring there was no time for pats; everyone was businesslike. He was well fed, but no one slipped him pepernoots. He wanted a pat very much. And yet, that funny hat was too much like that beastly bucket back home. Trendy backed away from the woman's outstretched hand. He even flashed his teeth at the hat, to remind it to stay well away from his own furry head.

"Wildes Pferd!" the woman said. It was a language Trendy knew he had never heard before, even if, no matter what the tongue, horses can't catch the meaning.

"I'm sorry. I don't speak German, like you do at your stables in Vienna, Frau Cavalry Master," the judge responded, smiling politely. "Only my native Dutch."

"Ah, it means 'wild horse'!" the cavalry master in her odd hat said. The judge's eyebrows arched in response. "Oh, don't worry, madam. We love them a little wild where I work at the Spanish Riding School," the cavalry master responded, sensing she had accidentally caused insult. "We in Vienna believe it is exactly what makes our horses able to dance in the air."

The judge smiled tightly. "Well, I am sorry to say that Trendsetter is not going to join your dressage school. He's going to be a jumping horse," she said. "You'll see at the keuring tomorrow, Frau Cavalry Master. He jumps more exquisitely than his grandsire Nimmerdoor. We would never let such a talented jumper go to dressage, where all you do is equine ballet," the judge said huffily.

The cavalry master looked at Trendy, tipped her funny hat at him, like a little bow, and headed off down the stable aisle, her tailcoat swishing behind her.

Trendy did not know that her unusual outfit signified that she was a powerful person. It was the uniform of the prestigious Spanish Horse Riding School in a country called Austria. That hat and that tailcoat were only worn by the best riders of all.

Trendy hung his head over the double door and, with a pang of regret, watched them as they left. He wished he'd let the woman rub his stubby forelock; it had been such a long time since he'd gotten a pat.

That hat wasn't so bad.

U

Sometimes stories go exactly as they should go. Tidy happy endings leave everyone smiling the minute the pages end and the two halves of the book's cover come together again, closing neatly over the words.

But life is rarely like that.

Often it is bumpy, scratchy, twisty, and confusing. And it's hard—when you're in the thick of it—to tell a happy ending from a new beginning, or a sad tale from a fresh start. It is important to know that the journey of life is never tidy and always a bit roundabout, so that you're not surprised when it goes topsy-turvy. That way, when it does (and it will), you can be resilient and ready to get it right side up again. That's a lesson every creature, including humans and horses, learns only by living it.

Day one of the one-hundred-day keuring was Trendsetter's day to learn that hard fact. For the first time since he arrived, the bleachers around the stadium at the Nationaal Hippisch Centrum were packed. Whereas in the weeks before small herds of the nearly one thousand young horses from every corner of the Netherlands had trotted, cantered, and jumped around the arena, today only the top twenty-five strode into the ring, the cream of the crop. Every other horse had been sent home. Perhaps one of those who remained would be so good as to earn the prestigious title. "Preferent," the people whispered in the grandstands, and no one wanted to miss that.

The sun was still low in the morning sky as handlers led the three-year-olds into the arena. Trendy, at the back of the pack, strode in a little nervously. Now throughout the seats a new word could be heard bouncing about: "Nimmerdoor." Trendy's grandfather.

"Look!" the spectators whispered as his rusty-brown coat caught the early sun. "Here's the new Nimmerdoor—but *better*!"

Trendy craned his neck up and around, taking in the sun's rays, the hum and hubbub from the audience, and the smells of twenty-four other nervous horses. Never ever had he seen so many people in one place or at one time; in fact he hadn't even known there were this many people on planet Earth. For most of his life, until he came to the center, his entire world had been the stables in Luttelgeest, his mother Olina, his best friends Kismet, Willow, Falkor, and a handful of soft white butterflies. That was all he knew. And now he was far away, surrounded by faces . . . so many faces.

And he'd gone without a single kind pat in an entire month.

That excitement—that vibrating stimulation that had thrilled him when he first arrived—seemed nowhere to be found. He felt empty there in the arena, in need not of pepernoots but of the kind hands that served them, the giggles that surrounded them, and the warmth that being fed the treats left behind. For the whole hard month before, Trendy had bounded over every obstacle, pleased to test out his strong young body, and intoxicated by his own whoosh, pow, and crack, as he leaped one towering jump after another. But now he couldn't remember whatever about the task had caused him so much joy and excitement.

If someone had merely stroked the crest of his neck or put a kind hand on his trembling side just then, Trendy would have jumped the moon for him or her. For here, truly, was a creature better than Nimmerdoor had ever been, full of talent, heart, and grace. But no one for the rest of Trendy's days would ever know that. Because just then and there, Trendy felt he had nothing to jump for.

And so he did not.

Try and try as the handlers and trainers, assistants, and judges would to coax him down the chute that morning, Trendy wouldn't budge. All he wanted was a gentle hand, a reassuring touch, and he would have leaped a skyscraper. But unable to express himself to the humans all around him, instead he just stood his ground. No one was listening to what he truly needed anyway, and that was the problem. As determined as he had been to stand as an hours-old foal, as stubborn as he had been back in Luttelgeest leaping for his lunch, now Trendy channeled all that grit into doing nothing. Nothing at all.

The shadows were slanting across the white dust of the stadium footing by the time the officials called day one of the one-hundred-day keuring to a close with a whistle. The audience rose from their seats and began to file out. Again the word *Nimmerdoor* was on their lips. But this time, it echoed with disbelief: "Nimmerdoor's grandson," they murmured, "couldn't jump even a single jump!" Trendy didn't listen. He didn't know he'd failed the keuring, that his chances at being a top stallion and at all the glory and fame that goes along with it were over. He didn't know that the farmer's hopes for the young horse to save the farm seemed finished. All Trendsetter knew, as he walked slowly back to his stall, sweaty with the exertion of staying firmly put when everyone had demanded he jump, was that he needed a pat, badly.

And so this time, when the woman with the silly upturned hat returned to his stall, Trendy didn't back away. He didn't bare his teeth. In fact, for the first time all day Trendsetter moved briskly. Right to the woman's hand, which he rudely butted with his head, and was rewarded with a nice, long, scratch.

"Not so wildes today, little Pferd," the woman said. "So you didn't want to jump," she continued, moving her gentle hands to rub the groove under Trendy's jowls, as the young stallion sighed with pleasure. "But that determination. That confidence. Even if you used it to *not* jump. I'm still impressed," she said as she stroked his head. "So look on the bright side. If you hadn't failed the test, that snooty judge would never have let you come home with me."

She clipped a lead rope to his halter and led him out of the barn to where a horse trailer was waiting. "I'll show you another way to fly."

Chapter Six

SARAH

As the young stallions in the keuring were jumping their hearts out (except, well, one), on the other side of the Atlantic Ocean, the girl named Sarah sat at her desk in New York City once again. As she sat there, she made an unusual decision.

Sarah quit homework.

By now she was thirteen years old and a seventh grader at the Clearwater Academy in Manhattan. Clearwater was a tough school to get into, but Sarah had received extraordinarily high marks on the standardized entrance tests; her scores were so good, in fact, that Clearwater had offered her a scholarship. Her mother, father, and grandmother had been so proud—and relieved. Even with Grandma Frieda offering to pitch in her savings from her past career as a secretary, the family could not have afforded the top private school's fees. With the scholarship, her family could breathe easy, and they happily sent Sarah with a crisp uniform and new shoes. It even left them money to spare, so she could keep taking her weekly riding lesson at Green Fields Stables.

Sarah held a secret that she had never dared tell anyone, fearful it would mess up her chances at this incredible new school: All those standardized tests that Sarah had aced, the exams that got her into this prestigious school, had an important thing in common: They were all multiple choice. With multiple choice, Sarah could answer all the questions—on math, on science, on the finer points of the English language—correctly, without writing a word. It was her favorite way to show what she had learned. That was because the letters did not get jumbled as they always did when she was trying to spell or form sentences and paragraphs. Filling in the bubbles, circling the right answers, Sarah was able to show how hard she worked, how much she knew, and how smart she was. She never had to reveal that when it came to writing, everything got horribly tangled and the words would not come out.

The thing was, Sarah *loved* to learn. And so it was with excitement that she had at first approached the afternoon's homework assignment. Ms. Claire Moses, her favorite teacher at her new school, with wild curls and a thick Scottish accent, had tasked her English class with writing a story from history. It sounded a little boring at first.

"You know I'm from the bonny banks of the Scottish Isles, and the stories I could tell you from my past! Of running amok with the wee Shetland ponies that run free in my homeland . . ." Ms. Moses began. Sarah sat up. Ms. Moses loved ponies too? "Class, you're going to become historians, but I don't want some tale of Napoleon's derring-do, or George

Washington's adventures—SNORE!" The kids around Sarah giggled. "I want you to research your own family's history and—here's the twist—tie it to history. You're all part of history," she continued. "You lads and lasses write your own history each day, with every single thing you do—or don't do. Now put it down on paper! Class dismissed."

It was Sarah's first big writing assignment at her new school, and though she quietly worried about trying to write it, the topic thrilled her. To Sarah, Grandma Frieda felt linked to history already—she was an immigrant from Vienna, Austria, and full of stories of her homeland! Sarah knew exactly the story she would tell. It was one Grandma recounted all the time. The story of how the pride of Austria, the Lipizzaner stallions, came to be.

As she trundled home from school on the M86 city bus that afternoon, Sarah laid out the story in her head, just as Grandma Frieda had told it to her so often. Grandma had made Sarah repeat it so many times, sitting at her knee in their living room, that by now she knew it by heart. Now, Sarah would just as often tell it back to her grandmother.

It went like this: Hundreds of years ago, on a trip to Spain, a royal Austrian nobleman, an archduke, fell in love with Spanish horses. Their hot breath, those fiery gaits, the flair with which they barely touched the earth as they walked. And when they pranced? His heart was stolen. When he left, the archduke took home the ultimate souvenir: a herd of Spanish horses. Stallions and mares, they left their pastures amid the olive groves for the white-tipped mountains and green fields of the man's homeland, Austria.

He stabled the horses at his estate in a place called Lipizza. There, a fierce wind, called bora by the locals, blasts gales off the Adriatic Sea. There were equines native to Austria already, of course. Battle horses grown tough in the limestone hills, called Karst horses. These animals bore gallant knights on their broad backs, and their coats were dark like the red dirt of the region where they roamed. The local Karst were as surefooted as the Spanish herd was flighty; as cool as the Spanish horses were hot.

Yet, as seems to be the way in great love stories, equine or otherwise, opposites attract. Soon, as if blown together by that Adriatic bora wind, the archduke's stable was full of a new kind of creature: half-Karst, half-Spanish horse, full of glory—and fire.

They called it the Lipizzaner.

The new creature that emerged from the stables at Lipizza was the bora with hooves—no, the Lipizzaners were the bora itself. And it was as if that great gust that summoned them into being kept blowing so hard, it blew all the red dirt right from their coats: Even today, nearly every last Lippizaner is totally white. And in Austria, they have been training them to dance since 1572!

The animals were so grand, so stately, that future royals decided they required a palace of their own. In the year 1729—Sarah remembered that year because Grandma would give a little quiz each time she told the story to make sure she was paying attention—an emperor named Charles VI built these noble horses a grand riding hall in the center of his father's hometown, Vienna. It became the home of the Spanische Hofreitschule, or Spanish Riding School, after that first foreign herd. And it still stands in the heart of the city today. It is made of pure white marble, with gold-dipped columns holding up a vaulted ceiling, and from the center over the riding ring, crystal chandeliers hang from red velvet sashes. Sarah had gasped when Grandma Frieda showed her an old postcard of the opulent hall. It was nicer than the Metropolitan Museum of Art and a far cry from the homey, dust-bunny-filled Green Fields Stables, or really any stables in America!

"That's a ballroom for horses!" she had exclaimed the first time Grandma Frieda drew out the dog-eared postcard from a desk drawer beneath the Sholes and Glidden typewriter. "Ha ha! Completely accurate," Grandma had said. "Because that is where the Lipizzaners dance."

The bus driver braked hard, and Sarah grabbed her backpack from where she had placed it at her feet.

She had almost missed her stop, she was thinking so hard to get Grandma's story right and plotting the paragraphs she planned to write. She stopped on the pavement and dropped her bag to her feet, unzipping it and pulling out a notebook to jot down details so she would not forget:

72
2
||
|
9

That was: exactly seventy-two white Lipizzaner stallions live inside their Viennese castle. There are two chief riders, eleven riders, and one assistant rider.

The last number was for the nine students—oh, how Sarah wished she could be one one day—called élèves. She smiled at the paper. She had written down the numbers correctly, without any mistakes. A good start.

Those riders train the horses to *dance*. The riding taught there under the chandeliers was not the simple posting trot and two-point that Sarah practiced diligently each Saturday. Wearing a uniform of funny hats with the edges flipped up, white breeches, and mud-brown jackets with tails, the trainers and students of the school teach Lipizzaners a discipline called haute école. Under the cavalry master's instruction, the animals learn to prance on tiptoes, twirl in place, and, in a burst of power, perform the most famous move of all: each white stallion learns to bound into the air, arch and stretch and buck into a magnificent aerial leap. It is called a capriole. To Sarah, it looked almost like flying.

Grandma Frieda had another postcard. She had given it to Sarah on her tenth birthday, and it now sat framed on the desk in her room. On it was a proud stallion mid-air, and Sarah had often peered and craned at the image, searching for the horse's wings.

On the pavement, Sarah also wrote down an important date: 2016. That was the year when the Spanische Hofreitschule, which, for its entire history until then, had allowed only men to ride and train its horses, admitted its first female cavalry master. Her name was Paula Butscher, and Sarah admired Cavalry Master Butscher almost as much as she did the Olympian Beverly Woods.

People hurrying home from work grumbled as they were forced to make their way around the girl standing in the middle of the sidewalk, furiously scribbling in her notebook, her backpack at her feet. Sarah looked up and mumbled an apology as a commuter stumbled into her. She smushed the notebook back into her backpack and skipped home to write the story.

At home, she skittered to her desk. She whipped out the notebook and placed it before her. Beverly's poster still was right at her desk, albeit a little faded with the passing of time, as was the little Breyer replica of her mount Amigo, now missing the tip of an ear, but no less beloved. The story was inside her, ready to burst. But Sarah never took out her pen. The words, the letters, the spellings, were already tangled in her mind.

She looked at Amigo on her desk, but that determined gleam in the chestnut's eye didn't help this time. This was not a jump she could vault, Sarah thought—there was no way to get to the other side. She looked at Grandma's framed postcard of the flying white horse, suspended in air. It was doing the impossible. She could not. She could not write the story of the Lipizzaners, one she was so desperate to share, or any story at all, without revealing to her new school her dark secret: Sarah could not spell. And how could someone who couldn't spell be at Clearwater Academy, much less keep a scholarship? When the tears started to fall, they did not stop for a long time. When she finally stopped crying, she looked down at her notebook. The numbers 72, 2, 11, 1, 9 bled together, wet with her tears.

There was only one solution, Sarah thought. To keep her secret, she would just not do homework at all.

Of course, she was wrong; in this life any problem always has many solutions. But when you're scared and sad, it is often easy to think that there is only one path before us. At the keuring, when Trendsetter refused to jump, he too believed that that was the only course of action. He, too, was incorrect; there were many options before him and many other ways to soothe the hard feelings in his heart. But it is the decisions we make that define our journeys. Right or wrong, Sarah and Trendy's choices determined their journeys and shaped their stories. And everyone's story is a thing of great worth.

That day, Sarah decided to quit homework for good.

She put the damp notebook away, reached for her phone, and dialed Grandma Frieda. When Grandma answered the phone, Sarah almost told her about her secret and her plan. But the words didn't come out. "Grandma, can I come over, and can you make me your sliced potatoes?" Sarah said instead, trying to hide her sniffles.

"A pile!" Grandma exclaimed in her lilting Austrian accent.

"And . . . and can I tell you your story of the Lipizzaners again?" Sarah asked, brightening.

"And the bora," Grandma said. "You must not forget the tough winds of the bora that made them who they are."

Chapter Seven

TRENDY

Trendsetter had never seen such a horse. Was it even a horse? In front of him stood an ice-white animal. The creature was so bright against the glinting snow of the pasture that Trendy had to squint a little to make him out clearly. The horse gleamed more brightly than the frost. His white head, with its curved muzzle, was cloud high. The almost haughty air with which he held it—his chin a little bit tipped up as he chewed strands of hay—made him seem as towering as the clock tower in Trendsetter's hometown. And the muscle that ripped around his frame made him seem built of brick too.

He was so imposing that, as Trendy stepped off the trailer after that long, creaky ride from Ermelo to here—wherever here was—though he badly needed to stretch and snack, he instead just froze. The journey had taken more than a dozen hours, crossing seven hundred miles of wintry fields. The driver was the woman with the funny hat. Though Trendy had failed at the keuring, the woman knew that that didn't mean Trendy was a failure. In her heart, the woman with the hat knew a lesson that it would take the young horse a few more years to learn: that everyone is good at something, and that you don't have to be good at anything, to be great at being you. And so she bought Trendy from the grateful farmer. It was a slightly cheaper price that one might have paid for the return of Nimmerdoor, but it was still enough to keep the animals back in the Luttelgeest stables well-fed for a long time.

Trendsetter needed quite a bit of refueling during the long journey to Hat Lady's (as the young horse had come to think of Cavalry Master Paula Butscher in his head) home; true to form, he munched through every last shred in the nets hung before him. Like all horses, Trendy did not have the ability to ever feel full. Really! It is actually a lucky thing when you mainly eat stuff like grass, which has so little nutrition you have to eat lots and lots of it to make sure you get all the vitamins and energy you need. Never feeling full is a bit riskier for a horse when it comes to rich foods such as pepernoots and oats. Since a horse is unable to tell when its tummy is full, it can easily eat too many treats like that and get a bellyache. Bellyaches are nothing much when you're a human, but for a horse, they can be a big problem. That's because of another uniquely horsey feature: Horses can't throw up! Ever! Hat Lady was very careful to keep goodies like grain and sweet feed locked up in front of the trailer, far from her passenger, since she knew if Trendy got his snout in them, unable to stop, he'd gobble a year's supply down. (To be fair to Trendsetter, any horse would.)

At one point in the journey, the van squeaked to the side of the road. The snow was falling harder outside, giving a soft look to all of the countryside that Trendsetter could see out the trailer's little sliding window. The ramp of the truck groaned as the woman, now in a different, furry hat against the cold, unlocked it and lowered it into the snow. She stepped into the trailer and threw a bright red woolen blanket over Trendsetter's shoulders; the rug was thick and warm, and all around its edges was elaborate gold brocade. "You look like Emperor Charles VI himself!" Hat Lady said as she clipped a lead rope to Trendy's halter. The halter was lined in sheared sheep's wool so it didn't rub the fur from his face as the vehicle bounced along. She tugged him toward the flurries outside, and Trendy shivered in his new red rug. They had been traveling for hours and hours, and though it was cold, he decided that getting snow on his hooves seemed worth it for the stretch. The brave horse followed the woman outside.

Near where they had stopped beside the highway was a bright blue sign, the words ringed in yellow stars. "Republik Österreich. Willkommen!" it said, as the Hat Lady read it aloud: "Welcome to Austria, wildes Pferd!" She reached between the horse's ears to rub her knuckles into the star between his eyes. "Trendsetter! We are almost at your new home!"

Trendy did not understand the phrase, but he understood a welcome. Everyone does! In horse, it's a bugling whinny. In human, we have words to replace the trumpeted neigh, but the excitement is just as catchy, and the meaning is just as clear. Trendy's fuzz-tipped ears pricked toward the Hat Lady, and the horse shivered again, this time with a little thrill. His ears spoke volumes too. They said: A new home? A new adventure? A new bucket of oats waiting around the corner?

"Yes!" Hat Lady said, as if the two were speaking plainly to one another. Perhaps they were, in the way that people who understand horses, and good little horses who want so badly to understand people, really can do. "A few more kilometers, and we're there." The snow sloughed down, sticking to the woman's fluffy hat, the horse's mane, and the bright red blanket. Just then, with a soft thump, a drift of snow slid off the trailer roof, landed square in the middle of Trendy's ears, and stuck there. He snorted. "Wildes Pferd! Your own hat!"

Trendy did not like hats. He knew just what to do. There, right on the side of the highway, he bellied down, and as the woman laughed, the horse sunk into the snowbank and flung his four legs up in the air for a delicious roll before they got back on the truck for the last leg of the journey. The snow hat was pulverized.

U

Rolling, stretching. That was exactly what Trendy should have been doing now that he had at last arrived at his destination: getting the traveling aches and pains out of his hide. But instead, all Trendsetter could do was stare at the blindingly white horse in the pasture across the driveway. He was glued in place. The strange horse's mane hung almost down to his chest and was braided in perfect coils, like ropes of silk. So was his forelock; it hung like cord between his eyes, to dangle smartly from one side of his face, where the brass nameplate on his halter read "Stellar." Stellar tossed his head, and the braid on his forehead snapped like a whip from one side to the other, his head lifted even higher. Though Trendy didn't know it, he was looking at a purebred Lipizzaner, a horse with fire in its veins and royalty in its blood.

"You put a red Spanische Hofreitschule blanket on 'im?!" a slender young man came running out of the stables into the snow, pulling on a mud-brown jacket with big silver buttons as he ran. His name was Charles-Isaac, and he was in such a tizzy that he pulled the jacket on upside down, so the neck was down by his waist, the rest of his coat still flapping and flopping. He glanced at the knot of a jacket he'd tangled himself into and started to fix it, still running toward the horse box. As he sprinted, he kept tugging, pulling at sleeves and fumbling with buttons, and tangling his coat more twistily until he fell headfirst into a snowdrift.

"Well, that's no way to greet our newest member of the herd, young élève Charles-Isaac," the woman said to her student. "Maybe you think he is our founder, Holy Roman Emperor Charles VI, and you are practicing a bow?" She laughed.

"Cavalry Master Paula Butscher, I am so sorry," Charles-Isaac sputtered. Humiliated, he pulled on the coat—his riding school uniform. In his hand was his own funny hat. He shook the snow from his curls, swiftly pressed the hat to his head, drew himself together, and saluted his teacher. "But, still, this horse is not a Lipizzaner," the élève continued, a clump of snow still stuck to his cheek like a frosty wart. "Even if he were white and not dark brown, I can tell he is nothing more than a Dutch Warmblood. Such a horse does not belong here at Piber Stud Farm, the birthplace of noble Lipizzaners. Can he dance on air like they can?" He was so upset he started to stammer. "This . . . this—creature—doesn't deserve to be here or to *touch* that royal red blanket!"

Trendsetter tore his eyes off of the glimmering white stallion in the paddock across from him. He knew that an argument was happening and that it was not good. Like all sensitive creatures, Trendsetter was an excellent reader of emotions. In fact, all horses can pick up on feelings; it is in their blood and how they are built. See, six thousand years ago, people first made friends with horses, trained the wild creatures, and invited them to join their human herd. But for four *million* years before that, horses were simple wild things. That freedom was full of bliss—and of danger. Out in the wild wide world were lions, tigers, and wolves. Wild horses had to think a lot about how not to be dinner.

So for those millions of years before horses ever had the safety of the stables and barns they live in today, horses had to be careful. They listened so, so closely to every sound. Even sounds as soft as a bird fluttering are important. (*What startled the bird?* asks the horse, upon hearing the rustle of wings. *Should I also be afraid?*). They developed keen eyes for shadows and were wary of anything out of place. They lived always ready to run, just in case that lump in the grass was hiding something truly scary. For all of those millions of years, herds of horse ancestors practiced and sharpened those skills. And thrived. You might say that horses got really good at reading vibes.

Right now, Trendy was getting a vibe. It was icky.

"Young élève Charles-Isaac! That is no way to speak about our new guest, Trendsetter," Cavalry Master Butscher said (though Trendy was having a hard time no longer thinking of her as Hat Lady). Her voice was calm and kind, such a contrast to the young man's that it seemed to melt the snow like Trendy's warm royal red blanket. From a lifetime with horses, the cavalry master had learned to think like them; she knew all about vibes and about how to make a creature feel safe and understood, whether that creature was a horse or a snotty young élève. " I think long and hard, élève. What is it we do at the Piber Stud? What do we practice here every day with our seventy-two Lipizzaners?"

Charles-Isaac was dumbfounded. Angry as he was, he was mostly struck by her kind tone. Pull hard on a horse's lead shank, and it will pull harder back. Let it slack, and he will follow. In the same way, her softness softened him. She continued. "Do we train them to be Lipizzaners?"

"N-n-no, cavalry master," Charles-Isaac said. "We train them in haute école, to dance in place in the piaffe, to raise their hooves into the sky in the levade." He paused, searching his memory for the fancy terms to describe the equine ballet he was learning. "And . . . and to leap into the air! The capriole!"

"Exactly, young élève. Well done. Here we teach horses to fly." She picked up the lead rope and gently encouraged Trendy to walk toward the glimmer of Lipizzaner in the paddock. Trendy's color was called *bay*, which means brown with a black mane and tail, and it set off against the silvery frost and the whiteness of the stallion across from him. The bay horse crunched gingerly over the snow, as the gray on the other side of the fence did too. Mirroring each other, the two horses gently reached noses out, the way you might grasp the palm of a new friend. In the cold winter air, they blew trails of breath into each other's nostrils, a greeting. The stallion stamped his hoof once, into a snow drift, to remind Trendy just who ran the show here. Trendsetter snorted politely, to tell him, "I get it! You're the boss!" And the stallion grew quiet again.

Paula Butscher nodded with approval at the well-behaved horses. "Young man, as the first woman to be cavalry master in four hundred and fifty years, I am living proof that even if years of tradition say otherwise, anyone—Trendsetter, too—can learn to fly."

Chapter Eight

TRENDY

All that winter, as the tulips lay sleeping, Trendy trained at the Piber Stud Farm, right alongside the Lipizzaners. And since all the élèves soon learned from Charles-Isaac's humiliation in the snow that Trendy was special to Cavalry Master Butscher, no one said a peep. Trendy made great friends with Stellar and the seventy-one other Lipizzaners at the farm; unlike humans, horses do not view anyone or anything as less-than. Trendy was chocolatey brown to their silvery white, and his forelock, still stubby, was nothing compared to theirs, which fell like curtains of silk across their eyes. But he was good and kind and great fun to romp around the pasture with, and horses see none of that other stuff anyway. They are better than that.

The young horses trained underneath the shadow of a grand cream-colored castle. It had a terra-cotta tile roof and a turret that tapered into a spire. When the sunrise flicked across its red tile, it almost looked like the clock tower in Luttelgeest with its funny copper hat. The sight comforted Trendy, who was doing his growing up a long way from home. The horses' days were filled with so much learning, however, that there was little time to miss Willow, Kismet, and Falkor.

As the sun crept over the cream castle and its red roofs, the horses would begin exercising. Each ani-mal had a designated élève who watched over them like a hawk, morning and night, cared for them, and groomed them. And, of course, because who could resist when it comes to young, brilliant, beautiful horses, the élèves fell madly in love with each of their charges. The horses and the pupils, you could say, were élèves together.

To demonstrate each day's lesson, Cavalry Master Butscher would take out Stellar, the grand Lipizzaner that had so transfixed Trendy. Stellar was as magnificent at everything he did as his name implied. His muscles flexed and rippled as he bounded in place, or leaped in the air, or—Trendy's favorite—performed the courbette, where he reared up on his hind legs and then hopped like a Luttelgeest bunny!

The most astounding of all the horses' moves, however, was the capriole. At her command, Stellar would launch into the air, and at the highest point, blast out a mighty kick, his white form suspended in the sky like a crescent moon.

"Now, mind you, don't get any funny ideas from watching Stellar," the cavalry master told her students the first day she brought him out to demonstrate. "Your charges are young horses; Stellar is a grand master. Do not expect them to be able to perform the highest levels, the haute école; we do not want them to yet! One day they will fly, but this takes time."

She snapped a little whip she held at her side to make sure the élèves were paying attention. They straightened up. Beside each of them their horses, young Lipizzaners transforming from dusky youngsters to the white of grown-up animals, with one nut-brown animal amid them, pricked forward their ears.

Everyone listened except Charles-Isaac, who had been grumpy the whole semester: As a result of his rude words, he had been assigned Trendsetter as his horse to train. And though in public the student smiled as he worked his horse in the riding arena, in the privacy of Trendy's stall, he grumbled at the young horse. He was angry at him simply because Trendy was not a Lipizzaner. Trendy couldn't understand why Charles-Isaac was always so testy, but he liked being brushed and loved the special Austrian oats he got, so he tried to make the most of it, even snuffling the boy's hair in an effort to cheer him up. Charles-Isaac just huffed.

One day, when Trendy tried to cheer him up, Charles-Isaac did something awful. As the warmblood breathed happy thoughts into his hair, the boy reached up and, without warning, smacked the horse. Trendsetter, for all the experiences he had had in his young life so far, had never yet experienced unkindness. Sure, there had been loss, as when he left behind Kismet, Willow, and Falkor; he had known embarrassment when as a foal he fell on his bum in front of his graceful mother, Olina. And there had been frustration when he could not convey to the humans at the keuring why he just could not bring himself to jump. And he had felt a bit of fear, at least at first, when he met the imposing Stellar, who ended up being as kind as he was regal. But Trendy until that point had never experienced that thing that slapped across his muzzle: meanness.

Horses are never mean. If they kick or stomp or even bite, it is only to avoid something, to express something, to get a message across. It is never, ever, for spite. His nose stinging with the blow, Trendy was so shocked, so betrayed, and so hurt inside—which hurts the most—that from that day on he avoided touching Charles-Isaac altogether and would shy away from the unkind boy in his stall and on the ground. No one had seen Charles-Isaac hit his gentle horse, except for a barn swallow perched in the arena rafters, and she couldn't report that meanness to any of the humans, even though she wanted to.

"It is not a failure if your horses are not stellar." The cavalry master laughed at her own joke, and her students chuckled politely—it wasn't very funny. "We must reward them for what they *can* do right now, just as who they are, and not demand that they be something they're not. Their best—your best—is good enough."

∪

No tulips came up at Piber Stud Farm once the frost fled. Instead stars of white edelweiss blossomed and bobbed across the paddocks by the cream-colored castle. Trendsetter missed the bursts of color, the paint of petals brushed across the landscape of his home. But when the breeze blew, the flowers danced in the pastures, almost like the white butterflies he once chased. By the time the buds of edelweiss tickled his heels, Trendy had caught up in the haute école of the young Lipizzaners. Despite Charles-Isaac's grouchiness, even he could see the Dutch Warmblood had talent.

One morning, the sun bumped up into the sky, and the sterling-colored young Lipizzaners each headed out with their élèves. But Charles-Isaac did not come. Trendy peeked his head out over his half-door with a questioning look, and peered down the barn aisle. There he saw Stellar, decked in his formal red-and-gold blanket, loading up into an extra-long horse box, led by the cavalry master. Then one by one, a select group of the young Lipizzaners, his herd of friends, each stepped up the ramp and proceeded into the trailer.

"I really don't mind that I won't be part of the performance in Vienna this year, Cavalry Master Butscher," Charles-Isaac said from where he was standing at the foot of the ramp. He shouted a little so the teacher could hear him inside the truck. "Trendy is not a Lipizzaner anyway; it would be embarrassing."

In her formal white breeches, brown tailcoat, and uniform hat with the turned-up tips, Paula Butscher stormed out of the truck and down the ramp, her face almost as red as Stellar's royal blanket. "Young man! Trendsetter is *not* the reason why you are sitting out this year's performance at the imperial riding arena!"

She was furious, as any horse or human could tell. "Your poor attitude is why I have decided not to have you join the other students. *You* are not ready, Charles-Isaac. When you realize it is you, and only you, who stands in your own way, then you will be ready for this grand event."

Trendy did not know what was happening. He knew there was upset and tension, but he did not know why. He did not know that the horses were heading to a performance in the most opulent riding hall in the world, the arena from Grandma Frieda's stories. The next day, they would show all that they had learned at home at Piber Stud Farm to a VIP audience in the Spanische Hofreitschule at the heart of Vienna. It was the very place in Sarah's postcard, an extraordinary riding ring of pure white marble, built by the Holy Roman Emperor Charles VI himself. The young horses would promenade beneath those gold-dipped columns and vaulted ceiling and beneath the crystal chandeliers dangling from red velvet sashes.

Trendy knew only one thing: EVERYONE WAS LEAVING WITHOUT HIM.

And so, one, two, three, four, he dragged each hoof backward in the wood shavings of his stall, reversing into its farthest corner. He lowered his head, he flick-flicked his tail—now grown long and luxurious—AND THEN HE RAN LIKE MAD. Right at the Dutch door, bunching each muscle in his flank, gritting his thick molars, clenching his jaw, and arching the crest of his neck . . .

Trendsetter landed in a clatter of hooves on the barn's cobbled aisle. He had flown to the other side.

The humans in the courtyard whipped their heads around at the sudden noise. Even the horses inside the trailer craned to see the commotion. When she spotted Trendy loose in the barn aisle, the cavalry master laughed. "You know what, Charles-Isaac? Trendsetter has just shown us he already knows the capriole, even if he uses it only to escape his stall! *He* is ready for Vienna. Gather him up and put him on the truck. You're coming too; you're his handler."

"You may not have earned this by yourself yet," she said to Charles-Isaac. "But Trendsetter deserves to go."

Chapter Nine

TRENDY

It was not the crystal of the opulent arena that scared Trendsetter when he and the other horses entered Vienna's Spanische Hofreitschule. Indeed, the crystal threw glittering light across the colonnaded arena, catching the gold-encrusted tippy-tops of the high columns surrounding it. But Trendy thought the dancing light looked a bit like the snow at Pilber Stud Farm looked when dawn broke over the top of its cream-colored palace. And so, the dazzling sight did not unsettle him.

Nor was it the formally dressed men who marched into the riding ring, each beside a full-grown

Lipizzaner decked in bridle work of pure gold. They were an intimidating army of horsemen, marching around the ring with the precision of horses in a carousel. But Trendy thought their precision was a lot like the way Hat Lady moved, taking deliberate steps that a horse could trust. Thinking of the hordes of horsemen that way, they didn't disturb him at all; they actually made him feel calm.

But that portrait on the wall . . . that was another matter. Trendsetter nervously eyed the painting of a stern-looking man hanging high above the riding arena. From under an imposing archway and high up near the chandeliers, the man, astride a white horse festooned with cloth of royal red, seemed to glare down at the young horses.

Though Trendsetter did not know it, the portrait was of the founder of the Spanische Hofreitschule, Holy Roman Emperor Charles VI. As horses and riders entered the arena, every one of the riders turned and saluted the painting, as was tradition. Trendy became more concerned. That man in the painting was clearly very important, but his frowning face looked to the young horse just like someone he knew: Charles-Isaac. And Trendy knew that for whatever reason, he could never seem to make that boy happy. After that harsh hit he had received from Charles-Isaac, the young horse could scarcely stand to be looked at by the portrait's painted eyes.

The Holy Roman Emperor was freaking Trendy out.

From the side of the arena, a gust of air swept in; the big gilt doors had flung open. In filed spectators, here to watch the Lipizzaners—plus one Dutch Warmblood—perform. The antique staircases creaked under their feet as they climbed up to the balconies that ringed the marvelous arena. Orchestral music swelled; the show was about to begin! To soothe the newbie horses' nerves, the élèves began to walk them around in a circle, at the arena's edge, and the spectators leaned out over the railings to "ooh" and "ahh" at the beautiful animals.

At the far end, exactly opposite the painting of the emperor, one woman leaned out from the balcony to peer at Trendsetter. The horse turned an eye upward. From above, the woman smiled down at him through strawberry-blond hair hanging softly on either side of a face framed by choppy bangs. Charles-Isaac pulled hard on Trendy's lead rope, hauling his head back down. In the balcony, the woman saw what the young élève had done, and she frowned.

"Ladies and gentlemen, thank you for joining us for our centuries-old tradition, made extra special today by the debut of our twelve newest élèves and the stallions they have trained themselves!" Cavalry Master Butscher said into a microphone, her voice amplified by a speaker directly under the emperor's painting. "There is also a special guest tonight in our audience, a world-renowned equestrian of the highest level, here to learn—because we must always be learning no matter how accomplished we are—from the Spanische Hofreitschule." Up in the balcony, the woman with the strawberry-blond hair and the gentle smile stood up.

"Welcome, all the way from America, Olympian Beverly Woods!"

A few days before, Beverly had just won the prestigious Grand Prix in Aachen, a city not far away in Germany, on a horse named Artax. The win had caused a stir because she was only the second woman to ride to that victory. She was in Vienna that day, on a well-deserved publicity trip, taking in all the horsey sights, as journalists from equestrian magazines, such as *Mein Pferd* (*My Horse*) and *Reiter-Kurier* (*The Rider Courier*), lined up to interview her. The crowd was suddenly excited. They were in the presence of a legendary equestrian. A cheer went up!

And then everything went wrong.

All around, the polished marble columns echoed the booming whoops and applause. Beverly Woods waved politely at the crowd, and the room of avid horse lovers cheered louder. The sound bounded between the columns, glanced off the roof, and ricocheted around the room. She made a gentle bow and took her seat, but the audience yelled louder, demanding that the Olympian stand again and be honored by their appreciative roar. The gilded ceiling shook, and the arena floor vibrated. Trendy rolled his eyes in fear. While the other élèves spoke soft words to their worried horses, Charles-Isaac spun around and yanked his lead rope harder. Once, twice, three times he yanked, hurting Trendy's nose with each cruel tug.

"Please settle down, everyone!" the cavalry master said into the microphone, seeing the effect on the young horses. Loud speakers, including a pair underneath the painting of the emperor, boomed: "Quiet please!"

To Trendy, it seemed as if the terrifying man in the painting was speaking.

That was when Trendsetter spooked.

When spooked, a horse shies away from strange (and sometimes not so strange) objects. It's actually often a good thing. Long ago, when horses lived in the wild, darting away instantly from whatever they could not understand kept them safe when the rustle in the bushes turned out to be a tiger. When you are a gentle plant-eater as horses are, zipping away from things that startle you, even before you take a moment to think about it, is generally the right move. Sometimes, however, a horse's flight instinct is not useful; for example in this moment, when the scary thing was not an animal trying to eat Trendsetter for dinner but, rather, a centuries-old painting he—absurdly—thought was yelling at him.

With a buck and a snort and a kick, Trendy danced at the end of his rope, and Charles-Isaac lashed it harder. That made things worse. Now Trendy wanted to get away from not just the noise, the painting, and the crowd, but also the boy—who should have been the horse's safe place. The other élèves stroked their Lipizzaners' necks and murmured nice things to them about carrots and sugar cubes; Charles-Isaac began to yell. Trendy was so startled that he leaped into the air, executing, though he did not intend to, a perfect capriole.

"Stupid Dutch Warmblood! I knew you did not belong here!" Charles-Isaac shouted, punctuating every word with a cruel wrench of the lead rope attached to the dancing horse's halter. "You are embarrassing the legendary Lipizzaners!" Tears of frustration and embarrassment formed at the corners of the boy's eyes. And with a whirl of his shiny boot in the arena dirt, he hauled on the rope attached to the frightened young horse, who backed up and snorted, the whites of his eyes showing in fear. Charles-Isaac reached down to the arena floor, scooped up a handful of the fine sand, and tossed it in the horse's direction to get him to budge. Spooked again, Trendy darted forward in panic, and Charles-Isaac, gripping the lead, ran alongside him and right out the arena door.

That was where Cavalry Master Butscher found them, after the other horses finished their performance. Trendy, now calm, was standing as far away as he could from Charles-Isaac at the other end of the lead rope. When the boy saw his teacher, he bowed his hat. "I'm so sorry that

Trendsetter embarrassed you, cavalry master," he said, sniffling.

"Wrong, Charles-Isaac," she replied. The élève looked up; the lead in his hand went slack. She did not yell, but her words rang through him. "It is you who embarrassed this great institution with your brutal treatment of a frightened animal out there in the ring. No amount of tugging and yanking and yelling can control a twelve-hundred-pound animal. Do you think Stellar performs the haute école because someone whipped him and pushed him to capriole? That would be impossible. It is his choice to leap; he does it *for* me not because he is forced by me."

Charles-Isaac gasped, and his face reddened.

The cavalry master continued. "Do you think our guest Beverly Woods ever forced Amigo to leap into the sky with her? No! She encouraged him *to choose* to soar." She continued: "This animal needs you to be part of his herd! To be a true equestrian, you must show through your actions that this place is safe, that you are safe. You must lead by example."

"That's ridiculous!" Charles-Isaac interrupted, snapping the rope between him and Trendsetter. "No one was ever kind to me while I grew up! No one ever 'encouraged me to soar.' It was 'Do this, do that, Charles-Isaac, or you'll get the boot!' and then a smack on the rear." His tone was sour with anger. Although he had never told the other élèves or his teacher, his life before the Spanische Hofreitschule had been full of cruelty. On the farm where he grew up, he had known nothing but grinding labor and harsh words from parents who thought that their strictness and toughness was the only way to make their son great. In truth, kindness would have made Charles-Isaac a better horseman and person. For Charles-Isaac, the big, soft animals he worked with gave him the kindness he had not found at home, but he had a hard time returning it. In some ways, he didn't know any better.

"And look where I am now!" he continued. "I am training to be even bigger than you and bigger than Beverly Woods. I am a future star of the Spanische Hofreitschule!"

"Actually, young élève, that is no longer true," Cavalry Master Butscher replied so quietly that it was almost a whisper. Charles-Isaac heard the words as if they had been shouted. "It is not Trendsetter who does not belong here. It is you."

Chapter Ten

SARAH

Sarah's no-homework plan, it is probably unnecessary to say, was failing spectacularly. (As you might have imagined, any strategy that called for Sarah to avoid entirely the very thing she needed to put her mind to was bound to go *ker-splat*. But in the moment, Sarah couldn't see that. When there is danger, a horse will gallop away without even thinking where its hooves may land. The most important thing to the frightened horse in that moment is one thought: Get somewhere safe. That desire to get away from danger is so strong that they will not notice that they are galloping through, say, scraping brambles, sharp stones, or slick mud. Sometimes a frightened person behaves this way too; sometimes all we want to do is run, even if we hurt ourselves in doing so.)

Boycotting homework was how Sarah ran from her problem. But like the fleeing horse who flings itself through the rough woods, her escape in fact got her into worse trouble. She started to fail her classes.

"Sarah, I don't understand," Ms. Moses said to Sarah on one particular day. "You're our top student, you can answer every question in class, and 'twasn't a day when you didn't have somethin' clever to say in discussion group."

Ms. Moses smoothed her skirt, and Sarah wished she could smooth the worried lines on her teacher's forehead too. It had been months of these kinds of meetings, and Sarah was sure she had put the wrinkles of concern on Ms. Moses's caring brow.

"And on standardized tests you shine, Sarah! So why, my dear girl, do you refuse to do your English homework? And your history teacher, Mr. Tokieda, says you're doing the same thing in his class. I've told you already, I'd have to fail you if you t'were to miss one more assignment." Her brows squinched together more tightly. "It just baffles me that I would have to do that with such a bright girl! Why, Sarah, why?"

Sarah pressed her lips together and shook her Beverly Woods bangs out to cover the thoughts in her eyes. She wouldn't let the truth out. She couldn't tell Ms. Moses that the words tumbled and jumbled whenever she tried to write. And as foolish as it may seem to someone who was not that girl at that very moment, failing her classes felt safer than telling her secret. A failed class she could handle, Sarah's frightened logic went, but telling everyone that she was a failure was too much to bear.

It was early morning, and the sun slanted in through the tall homeroom windows at Clearwater Academy. Ms. Moses had called Sarah in early to have this discussion, and the light reminded her of how the first rays slanted into Green Fields Stables, where she took riding lessons. She was so excited to be there because, in a month, her hero Beverly Woods would be visiting Green Fields and teaching a guest class, or clinic, as it was called. It was all Sarah could think about right now as her teacher pleaded with her. As things grew tougher at school, and adults asked questions that she refused to answer, the quiet horses, with their silent sign language of ears, were a refuge. They did not demand anything of her, other than that Sarah be a safe place for their hearts. That she could do, easily.

"I'm sorry to have to say this m'young lady, but with this behavior, I'll have to send you home from school." Ms. Moses stood up in a rustle of skirts. It sounded like the swishing of a horse's tail as it leaves you behind. Ice slid through Sarah as she sat at her desk chair, and she felt cold humiliation creeping over her chest. Sarah had worked so hard to be admitted within Clearwater's prestigious walls. And now it was kicking her out? For a moment, she felt like clinging to the desk, wrapping her feet around the chair legs and refusing to leave. She loved Clearwater!

But then another, unfriendly thought swept in: A girl who can't spell doesn't belong here.

Without a sound, Sarah nodded. She hauled her knapsack up from the floor and slung it over her shoulder. As she trudged to the door, Ms. Moses handed her a note to give her parents when they returned home from work later. "Sarah, I'm so sorry you're doing this, whatever the reason. Clearwater and I wanted to help you fly."

The tears did not come until the M86 bus pulled up at Grandma Frieda's apartment building. With hours until her mother and father returned from the office, she had gone straight there. In the lobby, she looked at the letter from Ms. Moses, still in her hand. She slid a fingernail under the seal and pulled the paper from the envelope. In Ms. Moses's slanty handwriting—the same scribble she used to praise Sarah's right answers on multiple-choice tests or to give pleased feedback about her in-class performance—was a message that made Sarah gasp.

I am sorry to
say that until she
completes the
assignments required
of her, Sarah is
suspended.

—Ms. Moses

It was as if a horse had kicked her in the chest. This was worse than just losing Clearwater Academy. She would lose Green Fields Stables too. Sarah's parents had said in no uncertain terms that if her grades fell—and being suspended meant they were as low as they could possibly go—riding was over. No more weekends at the barn, no more hours spent in the company of ponies who so completely understood her. No chance to meet Beverly Woods. She stared at the letter in her hand in shock.

And then Sarah did something that she would have thought unthinkable before: She crumpled the note and flung it away.

That was when she began to cry. She stood for long minutes, wishing there was the soft fur of a horse into which to weep. If she had to cry, it was always better to snuffle into the fuzz of a gentle horse while doing so. The thought made her cry harder: if they found out, there would be no more horses in Sarah's life.

When there were no more tears left inside her, Sarah wiped her face with the edge of her navy-blue uniform skirt. She glanced in the glass of the door, anxiously checking if it was possible to tell she had been crying. Grandma Frieda couldn't know her secret either, and surely she'd ask if she saw Sarah's tight eyes and wet cheeks.

She took a breath and pressed the buzzer, looking so forward to the warmth of her grandmother's house and the clack of the Sholes and Glidden. She decided she would ask Grandma to retell one of her favorite stories: the story of her last day with Modisch, the milk cart pony from the old country.

When Grandma turned six years old, her beautiful homeland of Austria was overtaken by a terrible force. These cruel people threatened not just war but also harm to Jewish people like Grandma Frieda's family. Frieda's family fled, leaving beautiful Vienna behind to find safety in America. They left in haste, slipping away in the dark before dawn. The plan was that they would head to the coast and catch a ship to their new life. They took only what they could carry, and Little Frieda tried to help, stumbling under the weight of her cloth bundle.

"Just then, there was a noise in the dark," Grandma Frieda would always say, her voice rising. "Mama and Papa and my brothers and sisters all froze like statues—we were sure it was the evildoers, and that all was lost." It was Sarah's favorite part in the story. "Then: *clop, clop, clippity clop*! I knew that sound by heart: Modisch! The milkman's pony was on her daily rounds."

When he saw his favorite little customer, her family, and their suitcases, the milkman pulled the pony to a stop with a quiet "Whoa." He was also Jewish, and he knew the danger their people were facing. Without a word, he jumped from the cart and called for Frieda's father, Sarah's great-grandpa, to help him unload every last bottle of milk and cream. "There will always be more milk," Grandma recalled him saying to her father, who felt bad that the milkman was leaving his cream to spoil in the street and tried to stop him. "There will never be another Frieda."

Into the empty wagon jumped Frieda's mother and father; her brothers and sisters squeezed around them and scrambled onto their laps. "For a moment, I was so scared I would be left behind," Grandma Frieda would say, Sarah almost reciting the story from memory along with her. "Then the milkman scooped me up, and—*plop*—popped me onto Modisch's back. I rode all the way to the boat like this, Sarah. We were saved by the milkman; I was saved by the pony."

Sarah needed comfort, she needed distraction, and she needed some of her grandmother's sliced potato pony prints. Sarah vowed right there that she would at least try, try very hard, to tap her grandmother's words out on the typewriter once again. Perhaps she could start with Modisch's story. Today she'd tell her grandmother her secret. Maybe her grandmother could help. Sarah pressed the buzzer again. Then a second time. Then a third.

Grandma Frieda never answered.

After a while, Sarah headed home. She had pressed Grandma Frieda's buzzer till her finger was sore, just in case her grandma was busy fixing a bubble bath or concentrating so hard on peeling potatoes that she didn't hear it buzz the first time, or the one hundred times after. But she never answered the door, so Sarah trudged home. Her parents would be back from work in a few hours. She decided she would practice how she would break the news to them and planned to rehearse the lines under the watchful eyes of Amigo and Beverly Woods in her room. She was still writing the little speech in her head when she opened the door to her family's apartment.

"Sarah! Thank goodness you're home!" It was her mother, home hours too early from work, her hair frizzed and her face frazzled. Sarah was surprised to see her father pop over her mother's shoulder in the hall, his eyes red. "Don't take your coat off," he said. "We're leaving for the hospital."

That moment, Sarah's insides were as scrambled as Trendy's on that terrible day at the Hofreitschule. Her heart bolted in her chest, her insides knotted and twisted, her whole being spooked. She understood in a second Grandma Frieda's absence, her mother's face, her father's eyes: It was her grandmother in the hospital.

The bad news from Clearwater evaporated in an instant; nothing felt important anymore. Losing school, losing horses, losing her family's pride, no longer mattered. Something awful had happened to Grandma Frieda! The idea of life without her grandmother was like being asked to ride a course of jumps without a helmet on: unsafe, scary, and impossible.

At Mount Sinai Hospital, Grandma Frieda was still asleep. She had slipped and fallen and bumped her head. Luckily she had been able to reach for a phone and call 911. To recover—if she were to recover—doctors would keep her asleep like this, for her brain to heal, for a long time. To heal, to succeed down the long path to recovery, Grandma Frieda would have to be very brave.

Sarah heard those words there at Mount Sinai Hospital, and a wave of regret came over her. Her decision to quit homework, to keep her spelling struggles secret, was not brave, she realized. It was cowardly. None of her heroes, Grandma Frieda included, would have behaved that way. Holding her grandmother's soft hand in hers as she slept in the hospital bed, that hand that scooped strawberry ice cream, provided for her family by working as a secretary, held Modisch's reins and led her family to safety, was strong.

At that moment, Sarah resolved to be strong. She would be strong like Beverly Woods and Amigo, who could fly over obstacles that filled others with fear. She would be strong like Cavalry Master Paula Butscher, who fought centuries of tradition and won. And she would be strong like Grandma Frieda, who, at age six, rode tall through the dark of night on a pony as brave as she was. "You are stopped only by what you can't get past," Sarah thought. It was up to Sarah to be the solution.

"Doctor," Sarah said, turning to a woman in the white coat at Grandma's bedside; the doctor was taking notes on Grandma Frieda's condition in a notebook. "Do you have an extra pen and some paper?"

Chapter Eleven

TRENDY

Giant metal birds swooped across the skyscape, and Trendy watched each land and take off with astonishment. *No, giant metal birds didn't seem quite the right way to understand them*, he thought. *Were they perhaps horse boxes with wings?* They roared in and out of the sky above as the young horse studied them with wonderment, so shocked by their uncanny flight that he sometimes forgot to keep eating his hay.

It was a few days since the mayhem in Vienna, and instead of going home to Piber Stud Farm with the

Lipizzaners, Trendsetter found himself trucked to this strange place of metal birds. He was currently parked in a horse box, underneath a sign that would have been very helpful to him if, that is, horses could read.

"Amsterdam Airport Schiphol. Animal Hotel."

"This is the one, Julian," a woman's voice outside the trailer window said. "The spirited young Dutch Warmblood from the Spanish Riding School, that Dutch Warmblood that Cavalry Master Butscher brought in to teach her students some horse sense." Into the window frame came first a man, and then Beverly Woods herself came into view. "You should have seen the height he got when he leaped in that *spook*, Julian!" she said. "He's like a young Nimmerdoor, a young Amigo . . . maybe even better. Trendsetter can *fly*."

After watching the incident unfold in Vienna, Beverly had gotten to thinking. The horse she'd ridden to victory in Aachen, Artax, was also a warmblood, a type called a Westphalian, and in Trendy's incredible leap, she'd seen all that same power. Artax had taken her to the Olympics in Seoul, Korea, where they had earned a silver medal. Maybe one day, with enough hard work, she thought, Trendsetter's raw talent could take them to the Olympics too. After the performance, she'd told her thoughts to the cavalry master, who quickly agreed it was an opportunity Trendsetter could not miss.

And now, the bay horse from Luttelgeest was headed to America!

First stop: the Animal Hotel. The Animal Hotel, however, is not what the name makes it sound like it is. And that's unfortunate because that would be so, so cute! There are no monkeys in bellhop outfits with little tassel hats taking a penguin's luggage to his room. There's no giraffe sitting at the concierge desk booking taxis for a family of visiting emus. It is, in fact, a way station for animals about to fly on airplanes. And, yes, animals often fly! How else do creatures like sea turtles get to their new homes in faraway zoos? How do African lions go to safari parks in, say, Florida? And how do Olympic horses like Artax go from their homes in America to Seoul, Korea, for the Olympic Games?

Beverly's friend, Julian Okwonga, was a specialist in helping animals fly. He had traveled all over the world with Artax and knew exactly what it took to get big, nervous creatures onto an airplane. He knew how to help them be comfortable on the journey.

Julian had a calm way of being, which came from a lifetime of studying these sensitive creatures, and he had gathered a ton of techniques for keeping horses relaxed in even the most bumpy flights. His pockets were always lumpy with treats, but his soul was also sweet. The animals knew that. One of his secrets was poems: He collected poems wherever he traveled in the world, copying them into a little notebook he carried. Whenever there was turbulence, he read the rhymes aloud to the horses in the cargo hold. They didn't know what his stanzas meant, of course, but they knew what Julian meant: gentle comfort and confidence. With such a person in their herd, they felt they could do anything. Even fly.

"You say this one can really fly?" Julian said to Beverly, laughing. "Because I'm about to load him onto this here plane, and if he couldn't fly, then I'd have a real problem getting him to New York!"

Beverly chuckled, and Trendy, though he didn't know what was so funny, felt through his fur and into his heart that he was with people as kind as the farmer, as Hat Lady, as the butterflies from Luttelgeest who had once landed on his nose and beckoned him to play.

"What's your plan for him in America? Taking him to your Kingston Stables in New Jersey, Beverly?" Julian asked, stuffing his hands in the pockets of his overalls. Trendy noticed then that his pockets seemed full of something round and lumpy.

"This horse is green. 'Green' just means he hasn't learned everything there is to know in life yet, as you know, Julian—big difference between naughty and just green," she said, and Julian nodded solemnly. "When I saw this horse kick up his heels, I saw so much talent in need of direction. My first thought was simply that Trendy just needs a chance to shine. Maybe I can be that chance. Thankfully, my old friend Paula Butscher allowed me to purchase him," she said, as they stepped into the trailer where Trendy was waiting. She looked at her watch. "Yikes, Julian, we better hustle. It's almost time to fly!"

Together they unclipped Trendy from the crossties, and Julian attached a lead rope to his fuzzy sheepskin shipping halter. Julian reached into his lumpy pockets and pulled out something that he held under Trendy's nose: A *PEPERNOOT*! It had been so long! And as Trendsetter crunched away blissfully, Julian led him down the ramp. He was munching so happily that he barely noticed when his hooves stood on the tarmac of Schiphol Airport.

Horses don't fly the way humans do, of course, seated nicely in rows with seatbelts clicked in place. They don't get to watch in-flight movies or get little packets of peanuts from an attendant's cart, squeaking down the airplane aisle. They do, however, have passports, like we do—documents stamped with all the vaccines they've received that mean they are healthy enough to travel. Trendy's was red and said K.W.P.N. on the cover. It was safely tucked in Julian's travel bag.

Trendy was still savoring the pepernoots Julian had stuffed him with when he was loaded into a giant silver box, inside of which was a horse stall. At one end of it was a net full of tasty hay, and Trendy got so busy with it that he barely registered when the silver box began to move. It had been placed on a conveyor belt and was clanking its way onto a forklift! The box had no windows. Because of that and because the box had truly scrumptious hay inside, Trendy paid no attention to the strange things happening outside.

He did prick up his ears when Julian's voice came through the box's silver walls, muffled but still reassuring. "Okay. I've checked his passport, and he has all the veterinary health stamps US customs require. We're ready to load Trendy!" he said. The box lurched a little, and Trendsetter felt the strangest sensation: that airborne feeling he loved when jumping fences or bucking with the bunnies of Luttelgeest, but curiously, he wasn't moving his body at all. That was the forklift. If he had been able to see out, he would have realized he was being raised up to the height of a Boeing 747 jet parked on the runway. Suddenly, his direction shifted; he was being slid sideways through a hatch that led into the belly of the plane.

The box came to a stop inside the cargo hold, where Julian was waiting to receive it. Julian poked his head inside to check on his charge. "Good boy, Trendy! Good farasi!" Julian said. *Farasi* meant "horse" in Swahili, the language of Uganda, the African country where Julian was born. "No . . . GREAT farasi! You're doing great! Now let's get you strapped in." He ducked out of view again and busied himself with thick cords of nylon rope, which he wrapped across the huge shipping container like ribbon around a present, tying the end of each to a hook on the wall of the cargo hold. "Nice and secure!" he said when he had finished.

When you're on a plane, it is important to be buckled up and seated for takeoff and landing. But Julian's job was to make sure the animals in his care were safe in those moments. And so, as the plane took off and Trendy's eyes rolled with confusion—*what was happening, this feeling of jumping without jumping, again?*—Julian stood in the silver box, braced against a wall for safety, reading poetry to the horse.

I had a little horse.
His name was Dapple Gray.
His legs were made of cornstalks,
his body made of hay.
I saddled him and bridled him
and rode him off to town.

Up came a puff of wind
and blew him up and down.
The saddle flew off, and I let go.
Now didn't my horse make
a pretty little show?

Soon Trendy was quietly munching alfalfa again. Over the next six hours, Julian tended to his every need. It was a lot like how a flight attendant serves human travelers from a cart full of drinks and snacks! Every so often, he offered Trendy a bucket of cool water that he poured out from a big plastic jug. When the hay net grew empty, he topped it up with fresh food. As they crossed the Atlantic Ocean, Julian dimmed the lights, talking gently to Trendsetter. "There's a time-zone change, Trendy, when we land in America," he said. "Rest up now so you're fresh when we land."

And so they passed an enjoyable flight together. Trendy snoozed and dreamed of the cream-colored palace of Piber Stud Farm, of the clock tower back home with its funny hat. Julian scribbled poetry in his battered book until THUNK! The landing gear deployed. But Julian was already scratching the white star between Trendsetter's ears when the startling sound rattled the cargo hold, so the horse didn't worry. Julian slid open a door in the silver box.

"Look, my farasi," he said. "Look at how far you've flown."

Trendsetter looked outside. Through a window in the 747's side, he saw an astonishing sight. It was as if a forest of clock towers and a million cream-colored palaces covered the landscape. But bigger. It was bigger—and then some—than Trendy's whole world up to this point. It was the skyline of New York City, and the horse had never seen anything like it.

But somehow it wasn't scary. Somehow Trendsetter knew he was home.

And yet.

The plane ride was smooth, but life was about to hit one of those bumpy bits in the road again for Trendsetter, those twisty-turny times that may seem like a dead end but are, in fact, just a way station en route to a new path. These parts of life are tricky because at that moment they really do feel like an end. And you can't be sure until they are far behind you in the past that they are in fact a beginning. (Though they are *always* a beginning to something new, different, and maybe even better, they rarely ever feel like that at the time.)

Trendsetter entered this latest lump in his life with his toe—specifically his right toe, the edge of his right hoof where, unbeknownst to his human helpers, it grew a little crooked. Horses' feet are not like human feet; they are a solid round block and hardly look like what we call feet at all. But inside their shiny hooves are in fact the bones that make up three toes—the middle toe is called the frog—that join together to form a round, tough hoof. The stuff of their hooves is the exact same stuff as makes up a human fingernail. It's called keratin, and like fingernails, hooves never stop growing. A specialist called a farrier, or a blacksmith, keeps horse toes nice and short, filing them into the proper shape every month or so and tacking on strong metal horseshoes to prevent the keratin from cracking and crumbling at the edges.

In his travels from the Piber Stud Farm to Vienna to Schiphol Airport in the last month, and now to America, Trendy's hooves had been doing what they always do, growing and growing. In fact, with no time to schedule a needed trim, they had gotten overgrown. His hooves were long. They were in need of filing and new horseshoes, and Beverly had an appointment with her farrier lined up for the day he arrived at Kingston Stables.

But first he had to get off the plane.

After the airplane taxied to a stop, his silver shipping box was lowered from its belly. Julian swung open the door to let in the breeze and lead the horse out to a waiting horse trailer to take him to his new home and his new future as an Olympic horse in training. As he stepped onto the tarmac, Trendy looked up at the airplanes flying overhead. He looked to the side at the city skyline just visible at the outskirts of the John F. Kennedy Airport, where he had landed. He looked behind him at the big jetliner he had just been inside.

With all the things to see, with all the looking around, there was one place Trendsetter did not look: where he was going. And that overgrown hoof, the one at the end of his right front leg, the one that grew out a little bit wonky whenever it got too long, caught on the tarmac. Trendsetter stumbled. As he tried to scramble to his feet, he stumbled again, that long hoof still getting in his way like a human might trip walking in too-big flip-flops. As Julian watched with his mouth open in horror, unable to stop what was happening, all 1,200 pounds of Trendsetter crashed forward, and the horse fell onto his knees. The horse and human heard a terrible sound: *crack!*

When Trendy got up, he was limping.

Chapter Twelve

SARAH

Sarah did not leave Grandma Frieda's bedside except to sleep. Curled in a blue-cushioned hospital chair in the corner, she watched over her grandmother as she slept and healed. But in fact, Sarah was very, very busy.

That piece of paper the doctor had given her turned into ten, into twenty, and as she kept her vigil in the hospital room, with her Breyer Amigo that her parents had brought from home, she filled page after page with words. She told the story of the milkman, of the evil people in Vienna who wanted her grandmother's family gone, and of the brave pony Modisch who rescued them. She wrote about the tricky dapple-gray pony at the lesson barn and his antics that made her scold him and laugh at the same time. She wrote about crisp potato pony prints, describing the heavenly smell, the sounds they made as they hit the oil with a sizzle in the pan. But most of all, she wrote about how each bite didn't just fill her tummy but how it filled her with her grandmother's love. And at last, she wrote the truth: She told of her bad decision to quit homework, to hide from her struggles, and her shame. She wrote about the Spanische Hofreitschule cavalry master and the Olympian who each inspired her to be braver and better. And how she now knew there was a better way to deal with her fears.

When Grandma woke up at the end of two weeks, Sarah was there at her bedside, and they looked deep into each other's eyes and smiled until it hurt. "Let's go home and make some potatoes" was the first thing Grandma said, clearing her throat, and they laughed with relief until tears fell hard. "Grandma,"

Sarah said, her voice catching, "how about I make pony prints for *you* this time?" In response, Grandma Frieda squeezed Sarah's hand and beamed.

Back at home once again, Grandma Frieda was weak but on the mend. She diligently did her physical therapy. "I'll be so strong, I'll be able to ride a pony again, Sarah!" she joked as she raised weights in the air or lifted her legs one at a time to strengthen the muscles. She walked with the help of a clunky metal walker now, but every day she was getting stronger.

One evening, as Grandma Frieda exercised while seated on the couch, Sarah took a seat at the Sholes and Glidden typewriter. Beside her were the twenty pages of handwritten words she had composed in the hospital. She put her fingers on the keyboard and began to type. Then she stopped. She gasped, and despite her promises, her confidence was faltering. The letters were still all jumbled, the spelling surely incorrect.

"Sarah, maybe this will help," Grandma said, walking tall and strong to where Sarah sat at the typewriter. She handed her granddaughter a beat-up text. It was Grandma's own copy of *The Horn-Ashbaugh Fundamentals of Spelling*.

"Oh, Grandma, I'm so ashamed! I always pretended the typewriter was broken when I struggled with the words. I lied to you!" Sarah burst into tears. "But you knew all this time that I can't spell?"

Grandma Frieda ran her soft hands over Sarah's head, brushing her choppy bangs out of her eyes. "No. Here's what I knew: I knew that you are the kindest girl, to humans and horses, the hardest-working and the best storyteller I know," she said, over Sarah's sniffles. "Being good is the hard part, and that you are great at, my dear one. The rest we can work on—together."

Sarah slid over on the typewriter bench, and Grandma squeezed in beside her. The girl began to type: D-**a**-**p**-**p**-. Sarah stopped. *Oh, no!* she thought. *How did the word go?!* Grandma Frieda lifted her own fingers to the keyboard. She typed:

l—e

And together they typed up all of Sarah's story.

After Sarah had left for her own home, Grandma Frieda opened a drawer in the typewriter desk. She pulled out an envelope and a packet of stamps. Into the envelope she folded the pages of Sarah's story, and in neat handwriting she wrote out an address.

Ms. Claire Moses
English Department
Clearwater Academy

She put on her coat, slipped on her shoes, and grabbed hold of her metal walker. She was still weak from her illness, but just like the little girl on Modisch the pony, Grandma Frieda was still brave. She put one wobbly foot before the other, and it was as if the bora wind blew at her back, urging her on.

With the letter in her pocket, she walked out the door. The letter was important, and no matter what, Grandma Frieda would deliver it.

Two days later, the phone rang at Sarah's family home. It was Ms. Moses and Clearwater's principal on a conference call. They had received Sarah's story, secretly sent by Grandma Frieda, and understood what Sarah herself could not: that Sarah did not need to hide, what she needed to do was to ask for help. Sarah's suspension was lifted, and she readily agreed to the terms of her return to Clearwater: extra writing assignments to make up for the ones she had skipped, and sessions three times a week with a specialist who could help her navigate the things with which she struggled. Her parents, who had grounded Sarah and forbidden visits to Green Fields when they learned of her suspension, were so overjoyed that as soon as they hung up the phone, they agreed that Sarah could start riding lessons again, as long as she stuck to the plan. The three of them wrote out a sort of contract about the agreement on a piece of paper, and each signed it in pen.

Sarah was so happy that she felt she might burst. There was a lot of hard work ahead of her, but she was ready for it. That Monday, when she entered Clearwater Academy, Ms. Moses was at the door, ready to greet her. Sarah ran into her arms. "Welcome! 'Tis so great to see you again," Ms. Moses said as they embraced, her skirt swishing around the seventh grader. "What are you looking forward to most now that you're back at Clearwater?" she asked.

"You know what, Ms. Moses?" Sarah replied, giggling with a sudden realization. "I've missed homework most of all."

That evening, after all the students had left for the day, Ms. Moses pulled out her own stack of envelopes and stamps from her homeroom desk. She was from a small island in Scotland called Shetland, home to the famous roly-poly ponies that bear the same name. As a lass, she had ridden on their backs all over the rocky isle, straining to escape the tight borders of small-town life. Though the ponies were tiny animals, as young Claire galloped over the moorland and the heather, the power they loaned her made big things feel possible. Those mighty fluffy creatures gave her the bravery to follow her dreams far from home, all the way to New York City. In the words of Sarah's story, she felt that flying feeling again; she understood her student to the core. And she wanted more than ever to help Sarah, as the Shetlands had helped her when she was a girl.

In her hand was Sarah's story, and a second stapled copy of it sat before her. She folded it and tucked it into an envelope. Then Ms. Moses took out a pen and wrote the following address on it:

Beverly Woods (and Amigo)
Kingston Stables
New Jersey

And with that, she put the envelope in the mail.

Chapter Thirteen

SARAH

Sarah shined her boots. She helped her dad iron her show shirt. She laid out her gloves, her belt, her helmet, and even peppermints for the horse she was to ride the next day, all on her bed the night before. Tomorrow, Green Fields Stables would host a guest that Sarah had been waiting her whole life to meet: Beverly Woods herself was coming to teach a clinic.

Sarah knew she would have trouble sleeping the night before. She stared at the image of the soaring Olympian on the poster at the far end of her room, wrestling with what questions she would ask Beverly the next day.

"What were the Olympic games like?" Perhaps. "What was Amigo's favorite food?" Maybe. "What should a girl do to one day jump giant jumps aboard magical Australian Thoroughbreds and end up on a poster on some future little girl's wall?" Hmmm. And while we're at it: "Ms. Woods, can you autograph this crumpled poster of you that I brought with me?" No, way; too gushy!

The dawn was peeking around the spires of New York City's tall buildings when Sarah drifted off, so great was her excitement. She had hardly slept by the time she was awoken by her alarm, but she wasn't tired. Time to go to the clinic! She pulled on the breeches and the sparkling boots, buttoned up the show shirt, and stuffed the peppermints into her pocket. She would likely be riding the dappled-gray school pony today, and though she was sure he would pull some shenanigans that might embarrass her in front of the great rider, she had now learned something important: Keeping your failings, your mistakes, your flaws to yourself was not a solution. Asking for help was a better way to go. If the pony acted up in front of Beverly Woods, it would create the perfect opportunity for the master instructor to give Sarah pointers on how to improve her riding.

Eight o'clock in the morning. Time to go. Sarah was too excited to eat and too jumpy to wait for the elevator in her apartment building, so she skedaddled down the five flights of stairs to the lobby. Outside, her mother was not the only one waiting in the car.

"Grandma Frieda! You're coming to the clinic? Are you sure you're strong enough?" Sarah exclaimed.

"Of course I am, Sarah. I've been exercising—plus all that work as a mail delivery lady really put some pep in my step." She winked. Sarah and her mother laughed.

"Just a moment, m'dear girl. Wait for me!" Sarah whipped around on the pavement. Skirts swishing, coming up the street was Ms. Moses!

"What are you doing here?" Sarah exclaimed.

147

"Well, you didn't think you were the only horse-crazy girl in our classroom at Clearwater, now did you, Sarah?" Ms. Moses said. "I couldn't pass up an opportunity to join you and meet Beverly Woods."

Sarah was overcome with excitement as Grandma Frieda, Ms. Moses, and she bundled into the car. It was already an amazing day, and she hadn't yet met a single Olympian! Off to the clinic!

At Green Fields Stables, Sarah blasted in with the speed of the bora wind, startling the horses in their stalls in her excitement. She ran to the silver-dapple pony's stall, eager to get him tacked up. But he was not there. Instead, there, ankle deep in the wood shavings and wielding a pitchfork, stood a slender young man. When he spoke, it was with a thick Austrian accent.

"Hello. I am making this stall ready for Ms. Woods's demonstration horse. Are you Sarah?" he asked.

Sarah was startled that the young man knew her name. She nodded slowly. "Then you are the one who will be riding him." Sarah was knocked back by the young man's words. The Olympian, a famous rider she had never met, had brought Sarah a horse to ride? And together they would be the pair to demonstrate her instructions and exercises in front of all the other riders in the clinic?

"He was supposed to be Beverly Woods's next Olympic mount," the strange boy continued. "But right as he arrived in America, he had a freak accident. He tripped as he was coming off the plane and fell on his knees. Hard."

"Oh, no!" Sarah gasped. "What a disaster!"

The young man smiled. "Well, there are two ways to look at that," he said. "Yes, he fractured one of his knees in that fall. It healed, it healed; don't worry!" he said quickly, seeing Sarah's face fall. "But there's no way he's going to be an Olympic horse, or ever jump the Grand Prix height. Those huge jumps would be too much strain. And he's not worth much money anymore either."

"So you could say 'What a disaster!'" the boy continued, trying to put on Sarah's same American accent as he said her words back to her. "But, on the other hand, he's got a good vet, and a great groom." He pointed his thumb to his chest and laughed at his own joke. "And he can have a long, chill life doing other useful things—like being a demonstration horse at this clinic, and your mount!"

"So maybe it was not such a disaster after all," he said, mocking her accent again, but his eyes were smiling, and she knew he was just having fun. "And just a twist in the road."

If the boy could read the shock on Sarah's face, he gave no indication. No matter what the horse's story was, she was still reeling from the fact that an Olympian had chosen *her* to ride him. But she could not share her thoughts; Sarah was still too stunned to speak.

The boy handed Sarah a bridle and pointed to a saddle slung over the stall door—her gear. "I know from personal experience that what seems like a disaster can actually be an opportunity," the young man said as he turned to fetch the horse he described from the trailer parked out front. "By the way, my name is Charles-Isaac," he said over his shoulder. "The horse is Trendsetter."

Charles-Isaac did know what he was talking about. That afternoon back in Vienna, when the noise, the fear, the painting all scrambled in young Trendsetter's head, many things happened at once. Yes, Trendsetter spooked, the Olympian saw, and Cavalry Master Butscher ejected Charles-Isaac from the academy right then and there for his bad behavior. But in the young man's words of anger at the horse, the cavalry master had heard something else—that in his young life Charles-Isaac himself had been treated as poorly as he had been treating Trendsetter. She knew that what her student needed was not punishment; like the young Dutch Warmblood, he needed understanding. He was dedicated to becoming a horseman, despite his tough upbringing, and like Trendy and all creatures, he was neither all bad nor all good. He deserved a second chance.

After the performance ended, when Beverly Woods approached her about buying Trendsetter, the cavalry master agreed—on one condition. Cavalry Master Butscher asked Beverly to take Charles-Isaac under her wing and teach him, as she would teach the young green horse, how to succeed. Beverly agreed. She needed a show groom on the road with her to help out Julian Okwonga as she traveled to Grand Prix competitions and to teach clinics around the world, and she trusted the cavalry master's judgment when it came to living creatures, whether horses or people.

And so after the disaster under the chandeliers of the arena, when the boy, furious and crushed, opened the door to the cavalry master's office to return his uniform and his hat with the funny corners, he found Julian waiting for him.

The animal handler spoke in the same gentle tone that could settle a frightened mare on a plane rocked by a thunderstorm. Charles-Isaac had expected more reprimands. None came. Instead, he breathed deep, the anger in his heart slipping away when he found no anger coming back at him in return. And then, as Julian offered Charles-Isaac a job, tears of relief and gratitude fell from the young man's eyes.

And so that day at Green Fields Stables, Charles-Isaac was there as Trendy's caretaker and Beverly and Julian's helper. He had promised he would learn from them, not just the discipline of the haute école but also the compassion needed of a true equestrian. He felt so lucky to be given a second chance at what he loved best—for he truly, deeply did love horses, even if he had a tough time showing it—that Charles-Isaac swiftly became the hardest-working groom Kingston Stables had ever had. And, after Julian gave him a paper packet of pepernoots to share with Trendsetter, the horse quickly forgave the young man, understanding, like all horses do, that we all try our best, even if sometimes we fail.

Trendsetter had grown beautiful. He was no longer the gawky colt wobbling among the tulip buds. Neither was he the yearling who leaped fences for oats. He was not the three-year-old horse who stood his ground when everyone told him to jump. And he was not the young horse who spooked spectacularly at waves of applause. His beauty had grown because his wisdom had too. His knee was a little puffy where he had injured it, but it didn't hurt anymore. And if he couldn't jump huge heights anymore, it didn't bother the young horse at all. Flying was fun, but so were many, many other things he could still do, and if he was a little slower when he chased those butterflies these days, it was still a good game.

His bay coat shone with an inner light there at the stables in America that afternoon. It was the light of a creature in harmony with himself, who was learning to accept himself as he was but would never stop striving for more.

Sarah was in awe of him as she rolled the pebbly rubber brush called a currycomb over his coat to loosen any dirt. It was brown lit with red, his legs fading to true black below the knee, down to hooves she polished until they shone like dark gems. His ears swiveled curiously at her and popped forward with delight when she offered him a peppermint. Between his eyes was that white—so white—star, bright like a thing you could wish on. In that glow, any injury or blemish disappeared. He was so stunning that Sarah felt shabby in comparison, even in her polished boots. She wondered if she could ever compare or if she could ever be worthy of such a horse.

How would she ever ride him in a demonstration?

Beverly Woods looked just as she did in the poster above Sarah's desk. (Sarah had decided it was a little too dorky to bring the poster along for an autograph, but she did have her Breyer of Amigo in the glove compartment of her family's car for good luck.) The Olympian sat in a tall chair like a lifeguard stand that looked over the riding arena at Green Fields, as the other riders enrolled in the clinic mounted their horses in the ring. As they mounted up, each introduced themselves and shared a little bit about why they loved horses and how long they had been riding with the equestrian in the lifeguard stand.

Charles-Isaac led Trendy up to the mounting block. At the edge of the ring Grandma Frieda and Ms. Moses stood side by side. They were beside Julian, and the three were chatting and sharing stories like old friends, about places they had flown and animals they loved.

"So this is my demo rider, Sarah, on my demo horse, Trendsetter," Beverly Woods said into a microphone, her voice carrying over a (not-so-loud) speaker. Sarah turned to the Olympian and offered a little salute, like she'd seen in videos when riders at the Spanische Hofreitschule saluted the painting of the Holy Roman Emperor Charles VI. Sarah opened her mouth to introduce herself, but she was cut off.

"It started with a pony called Modisch." It was Beverly Woods herself speaking! She was telling Sarah her own story. How could she know about the palomino pony? About the heart of Sarah's love for these creatures, about how much they meant to her? "I have read a very beautiful story about this pony, and about this girl, sent to me by people who think the world of her."

Sarah glanced toward Grandma Frieda and Ms. Moses at the railing and instantly knew what they had done. As Julian poked Ms. Moses with a friendly elbow, Sarah realized *they'd been planning this for a long time!* She blushed and smiled and didn't know what to think at all.

"It is a story about struggle and about bravery," the Olympian continued. "And though it had a few spelling errors in it"—at this Sarah grew hot with embarrassment—"it is the best story I have ever read."

Sarah reached down to stroke Trendsetter's neck. This uncanny moment, this instant where her hero was telling her that *she* was special too, did not seem real. The only thing that felt real was the soft, kindly Dutch Warmblood underneath her, and with his warm body, he seemed to say, "I am here for you too."

Beverly was not finished. "I have met someone else like the girl in the story, someone who has all the talent in the world and is ready to learn. But it is not another seventh grader. It is not even a person," she looked directly down at Sarah from the lifeguard stand. "It is a horse. His name is Trendsetter, this gelding right here." Sarah shook her head. Surely nothing so perfect and glowing, strong, and steady could remind the Olympian of Sarah. Sarah, who had lied to her grandmother, failed her classes, got suspended—in short done everything wrong, and who was only just now making it right? Sarah opened her mouth to tell Beverly Woods that she had it all wrong; they were not alike at all.

From the ringside, her grandmother spoke up before Sarah could say a word.

"You worked so hard for that scholarship to Clearwater," Grandma Frieda said. "And you know, I had a little money saved. She had been leaning against the fence post, her walker folded beside her. Now Grandma Frieda took her hands off the wooden planks and stood tall and firm. "I had planned to use it to help your parents pay for school. But, my Sarah, you earned your place there all on your own. And after Ms. Moses here had the bright idea to send Beverly your story, Beverly got back to us with a story of her own."

Sarah looked at the Olympian in the tall chair at the ringside. Beverly, the legendary Beverly, had spoken to *her* grandmother? About *what*?

Grandma Frieda smiled as she continued, "Beverly's story was about a horse with all the potential in the world—but who isn't perfect. Who among us is? And with that I knew just how to spend the money you saved me."

Sarah twisted her fingers into the Dutch Warmblood's mane as the next words were spoken; they were so stunning that she worried that she might topple right off the gelding, fall through the arena dirt below, and keep falling forever.

"Trendsetter is yours."

Trendsetter was just a simple bay Dutch Warmblood. For all his adventures and misadventures, his victories and mistakes, he was a good horse, and that was what mattered. And despite the wishes of the farmer, of the cavalry master, of the élève, and even of the Olympian, he was not a magical creature, a Pegasus from a fairy tale; he never actually had wings. He was content to try and fail, to try and succeed, as long as pepernoots were involved. All along the way to this, his forever home, he was one thing above all: himself.

And to a girl named Sarah from New York City, forever after, he was everything. She did not care if he could fly.

Author's Note

Everything in this book is true—the events just didn't happen exactly this way. Trendsetter is a real Dutch Warmblood with a stubby forelock, who was actually born on a little farm in Luttelgeest in the year 2000, and he grew up in the Netherlands surrounded by tulips and butterflies. And he really did fly to New York City in the cargo hold of a Boeing 747—I know this because Trendy is my own horse, and I have his passport with the stamps to prove it!

But in *The Flying Horse*, Trendy's journey to meet his Sarah comes from my imagination. Yet all the stops on his travels are actual places, and his guides along the way are based on real people, from the Olympians to the grooms. While in real life the Spanish Riding School in Vienna would never let a tubby Dutch Warmblood join its herd of Lipizzaners, the character of Paula Butscher is based on an inspiring real person who broke other barriers there: Hannah Zeitlhofer, who, in 2008, became the first female student in the school's more than four centuries of history.

Grandma Frieda is real, as is her love. Her family did leave Russia for New York to escape anti-Jewish violence in the years before World War I. However, she did not escape in a milk wagon towed by a plucky pony. That scene is a reimagining of the experience of my father, Dr. Yehuda Nir, a Holocaust survivor. He fled Germany in a britzka cart pulled by a two-year-old mare who carried him to freedom.

And Sarah? She's all me, from her mistakes to her triumphs. Like her, I stumbled in school, made poor decisions, and struggled with spelling—in fact, I still do, and now I'm a professional writer! All along the way, horses were my goalpost and my rock. They still are.

And so is Trendy, who, from his stubbornness to his crooked right hoof to his talent, is exactly as written in real life. And just like his character in the book, Trendsetter is my best friend.

—S.M.N.

Acknowledgments

You've actually already read the acknowledgments; you just didn't know it! That's because threaded throughout this book are the names of the real people and animals I love the most, who helped me write my own story. This tale is my thank-you to them for loving me back.

Thank you to Amy Novesky, my deft editor, who found me because she is Horse Crazy too; to my beloved Musa Okwonga, who taught me that a book could be about anything, even my passion for equines, as long as that passion was true. And to my mother, Bonnie Maslin, whose idea this series was and who loves me as much as I love horses.

And my gratitude above all to horses—I will never be able to thank you enough.

Keep reading for a preview
of book two in the
Once Upon a Horse series,
crossing the finish line in
Fall 2023!

THE JOCKEY AND HER HORSE

RAYMOND WHITE JR.
& SARAH MASLIN NIR

art by LAYLIE FRAZIER

*Inspired by the true story of
the first Black female jockey, Cheryl White,
and her horse Jetolara*

It was Cheryl's turn to feed the herd that morning, but every morning since forever, she had been at the barn at dawn, even before she was big enough to carry the pail. Back when she was too small to walk from their farmhouse at the top of the hill to the stables, her mother, Doris Jean Gorske, had toted her back and forth in her arms. Together they'd check that the racehorses had fresh hay and their water buckets were topped up, and then Doris Jean would head to work at the Ball jar factory in town. Later, when she was a toddler, Cheryl would go hand in hand with her father, Raymond, to check on the newborn foals or examine a horse with an injured foot. Cheryl couldn't imagine life that did not begin before sunup in the company of horses, not just because her life always had, but because she loved the horses her family cared for, raised, and raced, so, so much.

But her favorite mornings were when her father would lift her up and sit her atop his shoulders. That was when they'd head out to the field where the horses overnighted. Cutting through the green pasture was a path of soft dirt, a giant loop that ran at the perimeter, encircling many acres. That was her father's personal racetrack, beaten into the dirt over the years by the hooves of the racehorses he had trained, the racehorses his father trained before him, and those his father's father had trained, too.

With Cheryl atop the crow's nest of her father's shoulders, she had a bird's-eye view of the track. Her father would lean over the rail, stopwatch in hand, and together they'd watch as the men who worked for him exercised his racehorses. Dad would keep mental notes of each animal's development—

who needed to build their stamina just a bit more, who needed to take it easy, and who was ready to race. From her high perch, Cheryl also took mental notes: of how the riders held themselves in the saddle, how they positioned their feet, how they used their hands and eyes. That's because in her mind, she was not perched on her daddy's shoulders; she was astride a great thoroughbred, too. In her mind, Cheryl was a jockey.

Not that she ever dared breathe a word of her fantasies to the Raymond White Sr., her daddy, the famous horse trainer—he was the man who had bred some of Ohio's best racehorses, animals that had sprinted in the most famous race of them all, the Kentucky Derby. Jockeys came from across the globe to train with him. The air at the backside of the tracks where the jockeys mounted was punctuated with Spanish and French and German: ¡Ándale, ándale! Vite, vite! Schnell! Schnell! "Go on! Go on!" the jockeys would encourage their horses in their mother tongues. Raymond White's legend was so large that a prospective client once sent an armored Rolls-Royce to fetch him from their farm, shocking the entire village of Rome, Ohio, population ninety-three. (Well, ninety-four, if you counted Cheryl's annoying kid brother Raymond Jr.—which she didn't.)

Everyone called Raymond Jr. by his nickname, "Drew," which had come from his middle name, Andrew. (Cheryl, of course, told him it was because the name sounded like "drool.") Raymond Jr. was part of why Cheryl kept secret her fantasy about becoming a jockey. It was a secret she held in her chest even now at age fourteen. That's because Drew was a boy. In fact, except for Cheryl and her mother, Doris Jean, everyone who worked at Raymond White Racing Stables was male. Certainly every one of her father's jockeys was, as was every jockey Cheryl had ever seen at all the races the family had attended as they traveled with their horses across the country. The year was 1968, and at that time, only boys could grow up to be jockeys.

Cheryl had grown up riding ponies in the fields of the White family farm—fat Shetlands that were steady and kind and that she had trained herself. But she had never been allowed to train on a thoroughbred. Her father did not see the point: a girl could never race a thoroughbred. In fact, since thoroughbred racing began, only men had ever been allowed to become officially licensed jockeys. And that held true even then—in 1968—the year fourteen-year-old Cheryl met Jetolara. The year she realized she was desperate to race.

Jockeys have to be tiny. On her father's shoulders, Cheryl felt like she towered, but Raymond Sr. was in fact quite short, the perfect size to ride fleet horses. In most races, official rules allowed no more than 124 pounds, including the saddle, atop a young racehorse. Cheryl remembered the exact number from the jockey's handbook just as she remembered every number she saw. She had an uncanny knack for sums and figures that was clear ever since she first learned to count. On long days at the track, when her father had his horses and his clients' horses running in races from dawn till dusk, she passed the time playing with the numbers she saw around her on the pads under the horse's saddles, called towels: the number 5 on the green saddle towel of a lanky bay mare; the number 12 on the red saddle towel of the palomino balking at the starting gate. Using the numbers in front of her, Cheryl added and subtracted and divided, just for fun.

Flicking sums through her head as she stood on the sidelines helped her dwell less on how jealous she was of her father's jockeys. How impressive they looked, dressed in their white silks with the Raymond White Racing Stables' signature red polka dots on their sleeves and his monogram emblazoned on their backs: she wanted to be one of them.

Slim racing saddles weighed about five pounds, and the saddle rug was about a pound, so, she calculated . . . $5 + 1 = 6$, then, $124 - 6 = 118$. The jockeys couldn't weigh more than 118 pounds. That was why most of them were short like her dad; it is way easier to stay that light if you are small.

Drew was annoying, through no fault of his own. It wasn't because he and his pals pinged her with spring apples when she walked to the orchard behind their farmhouse to pick the fruit for the horses. The boys would hide in the gnarled trees, climbing up them to pretend they were knights in high towers, waving branches as if they were swords. It was a favorite prank: when they saw her coming, they'd pluck the tiniest apples from amid the branches, and drop them—plunk!—down on her, giggling like mad. Cheryl wasn't too bothered; sure, she'd holler at them for beaning her, but she'd collect the apples they dropped to feed to her horses, and in his goofy way, her brother made the chore a little simpler and a lot sillier.

What made Drew so annoying was this: Drew was eight years younger than her, but even at age seven—in fact, ever since he was born—their father bragged to everyone about Raymond White Racing Stables' future star jockey: Raymond White Jr., his boy. It crushed Cheryl that by the simple fact of his gender, it was Drew, not her, who might one day ride a great horse like Jetolara into the winner's circle.

If she couldn't ride thoroughbreds, Cheryl would find another way to stay involved with the horses she loved so dearly: she threw herself into the world of horse training. As she grew up watching from atop her father's shoulders, Cheryl used her mathematical mind to learn how to tell future legends from horses who would never win a race. Now her brain sped with equations as she timed the sixteen-foot span of each galloping stride the animals took against her father's stopwatch. She then divided those strides into the 660 or so feet that make up a furlong—the unit of measurement used on every racetrack. She flabbergasted her father and his jockeys when she didn't need pen or paper to figure out which horse was their next winner. When she grew too tall to sit on his shoulders, her father bought her a stopwatch of her own, and they'd monitor and discuss the family's horses side by side at the rail. That summer of 1968, Cheryl had reached her full height and had stopped growing. Her own numbers stood out to her: she was exactly five foot-three and weighed 107 pounds.

Cheryl did the math. She was the perfect size for a jockey. But Cheryl was a girl.

Each day, as surely as the sun rises and the cardinals tweetle it "Good morning," Cheryl's chores started over again. It was her turn to call the horses in for feeding time, and they came as they always did when she clanged the feed scoop and pail together as their breakfast bell: a riot of colors and hooves and snorts and whinnies from where they slept at the far end of the pasture. Savannah Lily ran, keeping everyone in line. She was just behind Jetolara, who was working up a lather to stay a horse length in front of the entire herd. He had been at the farm three months now and had earned the respect of the herd fully. He slept among them in safety and galloped with them in their joy.

Cheryl paused in her feed routine to give him his forehead scritches, as always, and he leaned into her palm, then stamped—a bit rudely, honestly—to tell her breakfast wouldn't serve itself, and he was hungry. She always marveled at how the horses knew exactly where to position themselves in the barn. After the frenzy of the run to the breakfast bell, they neatly arranged themselves in the aisle, filling in as tidily as students at Grand Valley were taught to line up to head to the cafeteria. Each horse ended up standing before his or her own bucket, hung by a hook evenly spaced along the barn walls. Each morning they claimed their same designated spot and guarded it vigilantly.

Clever Jeto had done one better—he had managed to claim the feed pail that hung directly below the trap door to the hayloft above. That was where Cheryl would do her next chore: throwing down flakes from the big bales of timothy and alfalfa stored up there to the hungry horses below. In that spot, Jeto had a front-row seat: when the hay came raining down, he would be the first to grab a mouthful.

Every pail full with oats, the horses crunching happily in the barn below, Cheryl climbed the sawdusty ladder up to the loft. It was peaceful up there, and sometimes she would take a break here. She would count the hundreds of rays of slanting light that slipped through cracks in the timber framing, the dust sparkling through them, and multiply them as if they were tally sticks. Today hay was piled to the roof—a new shipment had been stacked the night before—and she began to count them and multiply them, getting lost in numbers and the cheeps of the cardinals who nested in among the bales.

Then she heard it. It wasn't the trill of her state's beloved bird, the little song that flitted around the farm and was such a part of Raymond White Racing Stables that her father's jockeys wore silks of red—Cardinal red—as they rode. It was a bird's cry of pain.

Worried, Cheryl cast about among the bales, looking high in the eaves of the hayloft and low through the cracks in the floor for the distressed bird. Then she spotted it: halfway to the ceiling, in a tower of bales just beside the trap door was a blur of red fluttering.

A cardinal—its wing pinioned between two massive bales of alfalfa—must have been caught flying across the loft as the workmen flung the heavy loads of hay into stacks.

Quick as a filly out of the gate, Cheryl raced to the rescue. She hooked her fingers into the baling twine that wrapped each bale and climbed up the tower of hay to where the precious little bird was helplessly flit-flitting and cheep-cheeping. When she got to it, ever-so-gently so as not to crush the creature, she pried up the bale on top and then pushed it slightly back, freeing the wing. In that instant, the wisp of a bird looked deep into Cheryl's eye with its own black bead. Cheryl felt an unspoken thank-you just before the bird flew away, unharmed.

Then the tower of hay toppled.

Cheryl was falling, tumbling, bracing to hit the slatted hayloft floor and surely get the wind knocked out of her. But she did not. Because right below her was that trap door.

And right below that trap door was Jetolara.

She landed on his back with a thud, his withers slamming into her chest. The breath disappeared from her lungs, and she reached almost instinctively to wrap her arms around his neck. To the thoroughbred beneath her, whatever had just landed on his back did so just as a coyote would have, clamping onto his shoulders and, he thought wildly, trying to make him prey. And so Jetolara did what his cells and sinews and bones and breath had for generations told him would bring him to safety: he ran.

The chestnut galloped out of the barn with Cheryl clinging to his back, still unable to catch her breath. He flew down the pasture, his hooves trampling Drew's baseball diamond. He blasted past the buckeye tree and, alongside the Ohio River, outpaced the current with every bounding leap. When he hit the track on which Cheryl's great-great-grandfather had ridden horses, and every man in the White family since him had too, he did what thoroughbreds do best: Jetolara raced. Cheryl was gasping now, braiding her fingers into his rust-red mane, hugging her strong legs around him—he was going too fast to risk falling off—and becoming aware of shouts coming from the family farmhouse. Her father screaming, "Stop! Oh, dear Lord, Doris Jean! It's Cheryl! And Jeto! JETOLARA, STOP!"

Without a bridle or a saddle, Cheryl could no more stop the careening thoroughbred than she could stop a cardinal from singing. But as her breath steadied, and the warm back of the animal plunged and coiled beneath her, she realized—she did not want to stop. She was a jockey—at last! All that careful study of her father's riders meant she knew what to do. As Jeto ran wild, she mimicked their position. She pushed her chest up from his withers and squared her shoulders, tucked up her legs, and shoved her heels down. As he sped down the furlongs, she shifted her seat to the center of his back and in a steady voice said: "Jetolara, it's me, Cheryl."

The fear in the horse's chest parted like clouds at the sound of his girl's voice. The visions of a coyote, a bobcat, or a danger melted away, and he steadied his canter. Then he bounced to an easy trot. Then Jetolara stopped, turned back to look at his rider, and plainly begged her for some oats.

Huffing and sweating, her father arrived at the paddock's edge, her mother swift behind him, their faces ashen with worry. Cheryl dismounted. Jetolara followed her to them without so much as a lead rope, like a puppy, as she explained what had happened.

Then she startled them, perhaps herself most of all, with what she said next. "Papa, I love myself. And I'm going to be a jockey," she said, reaching up to scratch Jetolara's long white stripe. "In fact, I already am."

SARAH MASLIN NIR is a Pulitzer Prize–nominated reporter for the *New York Times* and the author of the adult memoir, *Horse Crazy: The Story of a Woman and a World in Love with an Animal.* Second only to Sarah's love of horses, which she has been riding and showing since the age of two, is her love of horse books. *The Flying Horse* is her first novel for young readers. She lives in New York City.

The cover and spot art for this book were created by LAYLIE FRAZIER, a fine artist and illustrator who lives in Houston, Texas. Laylie doesn't ride horses, but she loves to illustrate them.